Out of the mist and smoke, a dead man strode towards her, keeping close to the wall, staying in the shadows.

But coming. For her. Natalie began to shake. Shots rang out. Crouching, the man began to run. But so far, he hadn't been hit. He'd always been lucky that way. At least until the day he'd died.

When he reached her, he stopped, a hint of wariness in his gaze.

"Either I'm dying, dead. Or you're not dead," she said, feeling like an idiot, still not sure what to think.

His dark gaze locked with hers, daring her wrath. "I'm not dead."

"Sean." Fierce joy rose in her. Joy and disbelief and…anger! Anger, fury, rage. Hard and hot, pushing away everything else.

Two years ago, she'd been angry with him for dying. For leaving her. Now she was enraged to learn that he'd lived…

Dear Reader,

After writing *The Princess's Secret Scandal* for the CAPTURING THE CROWN series. I knew there were stories yet untold. Most of the other authors felt the same way, so we got together and proposed another series, MISSION: IMPASSIONED. *Bulletproof Marriage* is my contribution.

Marriage is complicated and wonderful, dangerous and safe, passionate and serene. Because my own marriage is so awesome, I know that love truly can carry on despite bad times and troubles. When Sean McGregor told me his story and how much he loved his wife, I knew I'd found my story. I sympathised with both Sean and Natalie, and longed to help them find each other again.

I hope you enjoy sharing danger and love with these two super-spies! I sure did.

Sincerely,

Karen Whiddon

Bulletproof Marriage

KAREN WHIDDON

MILLS & BOON

Pure reading pleasure

First published in Great Britain 2008
by Harlequin Mills & Boon Limited,
Eton House, 18-24 Paradise Road, Richmond, Surrey TW9 1SR

© Karen Whiddon 2007

ISBN: 978 0 263 86004 7

46-1108

Harlequin Mills & Boon policy is to use papers that are
natural, renewable and recyclable products and made from
wood grown in sustainable forests. The logging and
manufacturing processes conform to the legal environmental
regulations of the country of origin.

Printed and bound in Spain
by Litografia Rosés S.A., Barcelona

ABOUT THE AUTHOR

Karen Whiddon started weaving fanciful tales for her younger brothers at the age of eleven. Amid the Catskill Mountains of New York, then the Rocky Mountains of Colorado, she fuelled her imagination with the natural beauty of the rugged peaks and spun stories of love that captivated her family's attention.

Karen now lives in north Texas, where she shares her life with her very own hero of a husband and three doting dogs. Also an entrepreneur, she divides her time between the business she started and writing the contemporary romantic suspense and paranormal romances that readers enjoy. You can e-mail Karen at KWhiddon1@aol.com or write to her at PO Box 820807, Fort Worth, TX 76182, USA. Fans of her writing can also check out her website at www.KarenWhiddon.com.

For Daisy, Mitchell and Mac, my four-legged
writing companions and fur-faced children.

Chapter 1

If reinforcements didn't show up soon, Natalie Major thought grimly, she might as well paint a target on her chest and leap into the open. The unknown assassin—or assassins—were that close. The decaying concrete warehouse she'd holed up in only had two ways out—and one of them had been blown to rubble.

She needed help. Corbett Lazlo, her father's oldest friend and owner of one of the top private investigative agencies in the world, had promised to send someone. She'd asked for the best.

Now she wished she'd asked for the most prompt.

Gallows humor. She'd never been particularly good at it before, though she'd grown more proficient.

Her husband wouldn't even recognize her now if he were still alive. Once, he'd been Lazlo's top agent. She'd married a Lazlo Group spook, just like her own father had been. Retired now, and in a wheelchair, her father lived in relative seclusion. Her beloved husband, Sean, hadn't been so lucky. He'd been killed two years ago this week. Lazlo's group seemed to be the ruin of everyone she loved, so in honor of her dead husband and disabled father, and in defiance of the Lazlo legacy she could easily have embraced, she'd worked her way to the top of SIS, the British Secret Intelligence Service. There was no job too difficult, no task too dangerous for Sean McGregor's widow.

Until now.

She scouted the area. Trapped inside the abandoned warehouse, she was fast running out of options. The concrete walls made a good shield against bullets, but she needed to see her enemies. Right now, she could only hear them. And it was hard to fight when you had no idea who the enemy might be. Or where they were hiding.

Plus, cement was cold and hard and reminded her too damn much of a tomb.

The shooters fired off another round of shots. AK-47s. Random bullets ricocheted crazily and dangerously off the cement walls and floors. She couldn't even dodge them, having no idea where they'd go.

She'd found the abandoned warehouse two days

ago. A concrete bunker in a run-down area of Glasgow had seemed relatively safe. Not wanting to endanger others by staying at a B and B or hotel, she'd used the concrete warehouse as her base, returning to sleep and regroup while attempting to gather information on whoever had sold out her team. Since Millaflora—a low-down, no-good mole operating as a double agent inside the SIS—had already been caught, she had no idea who she was looking for.

Officially, she was on administrative leave, supposedly holed up, incognito in an unknown luxury hotel on the French Riviera. No one in her office knew she'd come to Glasgow, not even her supervisor.

And though she'd tried to take extraordinary precautions similar to those she used when deep undercover, her enemy had found her.

Whoever "they" were.

She supposed the whys and the hows didn't matter. Not now. All that mattered was that if help didn't arrive soon, she was dead.

Her ammo nearly gone, no backup, and no alternative plan—pretty shoddy situation for an undercover agent who'd recently been promoted to team leader.

It had to have something to do with the code. Natalie was sure of it. She'd been so close to cracking it. She and her team.

Now they all were dead and she was on the run.

And she had only herself to rely on. In seven years of service, she'd never had a single casualty. Until now. Now she'd lost her entire team. They'd been eliminated, killed in a way that left no doubt she was next. All the codes they'd been working on had disappeared, at least as far as anyone knew. She'd told no one that she'd made her own private copy.

Not knowing who was on her side, she hadn't dared to contact SIS. She'd called her father, knowing he'd contact Corbett, knowing Lazlo would help.

"Come on, reinforcements," she muttered. Her father'd told her Corbett had promised to send help. The head of the Lazlo Group never went back on his word.

A movement across the alley caught her attention. Finally! Someone had arrived to help her out of this hellhole.

She took another look and blinked, wondering if the stress had finally claimed her mind.

Out of the mist and smoke, a dead man strode toward her, keeping close to the wall, staying in the shadows, but coming. For her.

Natalie began to shake.

Shots rang out. Crouching, the man began to run. More shots. So far, he hadn't been hit. He'd always been lucky that way.

At least, until the day he'd died.

Dead. He was dead and buried.

Rocking back onto her heels, she rubbed her eyes and took another look.

She hadn't been wrong. The man she'd loved more than any other, her soul mate, her husband, the man she'd mourned, the man she'd never thought to see again, kept moving toward her.

Frozen, she watched as he continued, his low crouch purposeful and unafraid. Or maybe he didn't care. After all, a man couldn't die twice, right?

Her heart drummed in her ears. Sean. Her husband, Sean. This couldn't be real, couldn't be happening.

She wasn't the type to faint—not anymore. Too many hard lessons learned. Instead, she'd taught herself to push back, to fight.

But how did one battle a ghost?

From the smoke and the grave, against the periodic bursts of gunfire, he continued to come toward her. He moved exactly the way she remembered—purposeful and bold, dodging bullets as though he were untouchable. She'd often thought that very arrogance had been what had gotten him killed.

Killed.

Yet here he was, ducking under the concrete overhang into her shadowed hiding place, solid and real and alive.

When he reached her, he stopped, his dark gaze intense. She couldn't move. He was still beautiful, even in the dust and the dirt and the danger. She caught her breath, unable to speak.

"I'm here," he said, his voice husky, as though too long unused, a hint of wariness in his gaze.

"I…" She moved toward him, inspecting him, still unable to believe what the fates had just returned to her.

"Get down," he snarled, yanking her behind the concrete wall with him as the shooters let loose with several rounds of shots.

"What the—" he cursed, letting her go. "They've got AK-47s. You must have royally pissed someone off. Why are they trying to kill you?"

She still couldn't find her voice. Unable to help herself, she let her gaze roam hungrily over his muscular body—the way her hands used to.

"Either I'm dead, dying or you're not dead," she said, feeling like an idiot, still not sure what to think.

"No." His dark gaze locked with hers, daring her wrath. "I'm not dead."

"Sean." Fierce joy rose in her. Joy and disbelief and…anger. Anger, fury, rage. Hard and hot, pushing away everything else. "I went to your funeral. You died in a car crash on your way to the airport."

He dragged his hand through his hair. "It was set up," he said, unsmiling. "I went into hiding. But your father called Corbett, who told me you were in trouble. I've come to help."

To help. Not because he loved her or missed her, but because his boss had requested it. Of course.

Anyone who'd pretend to die, who'd let his wife grieve and mourn…

Speechless, all she could do was shake her head. Then suddenly, tears streamed down her cheeks as she began to weep, crying in great big, gasping sobs.

Another round of shots rang out. They both ignored them.

"Don't." Reaching for her, his expression looked pained, and she remembered how he'd always hated it when she'd cried. He'd welcome a fight, maybe even a discussion, but he'd never been able to deal with a woman's tears. Or, more specifically, hers.

Suddenly, she hated him. "Stay away from me."

"But I—"

"No." Still crying, she felt rage again knife through her, chasing away the pain. Blinding fury, the kind she'd had to draw upon again and again to get through her grief.

Then, she'd been angry with him for dying. For leaving her. Now, she was enraged to learn he'd lived.

She looked lovelier than he'd remembered, which shouldn't be possible. Her face had haunted his dreams each and every night of the two years they'd been apart. He'd kept track of her from a distance, relying on Corbett Lazlo to keep him up to date.

Now, he stood before the woman he hadn't seen in two long years, the woman he'd never stopped loving, and prepared to face her wrath. After all, he'd expected it, and God knows he deserved it.

Another round of gunshots shattered the concrete floor in front of them.

"This way." Grabbing her, Sean dove deeper inside the building.

Because she had no choice, she went with him. "What are you doing? I've walked the perimeter—there is no other door. We'll be trapped."

"Yes there is. You must have missed it. I had the satellite check out this place before I got here. There's another way out, though it's on the other side of the shipping area. This warehouse has apparently been abandoned for a long time. Vandals have busted out the back loading doors."

"How do you know the shooters won't already be there?" Despite her question, she shook off his grip and pushed ahead of him. When she glanced over her shoulder to make sure he followed, her face was absolutely expressionless. Not the fury he'd expected, not even sorrow. Instead, she had the cold, calculating look of a seasoned undercover agent, one prepared to do what had to be done to make it out alive.

"I don't. Where's your backup?" he asked her.

"I don't have any. I'm not supposed to be here."

"What?"

Ignoring him, she kept moving.

Wary, he stayed close behind her. This was Natalie, and knowing how much his return from the grave must have shocked her he wasn't sure what to expect.

More gunfire, closer this time. "They're moving in," he said. She didn't respond.

He grabbed her arm. "Nat, stop."

Her eyes narrowed and he braced himself for the storm.

Instead, face blank, she looked at him and shook her head, as though she found him wanting. "I would suggest," she said, her voice deadly calm, "that you let go of me. If you don't want to go with me, then turn around and go back to whatever rock you crawled out from under."

Ah, now this was the Natalie he knew. "Let's postpone this discussion for after we've gotten out of here alive, don't you think?"

Immediately she nodded. "Of course. Forgive me. I wasn't aware there was a code of conduct for how a wife is supposed to act when learning her beloved husband had faked his death and not only lied to her, but voluntarily spent the past two years away from her."

He glared back. "There isn't. But there *is* a code of conduct for staying alive. *Move!*"

"Right." She lifted her chin and took off.

More gunshots. "What the hell are they doing, shooting randomly in the dark?" He cursed. "They'll hit their own men with the ricocheting bullets. Stupid idiots."

The blackness had become absolute. And he didn't dare light a match. Hands out before him, he felt his way, concrete pillar by concrete pillar.

"I hope you're right about this exit. If you're wrong, we're trapped here."

"Satellite photos are pretty accurate. There should be another hallway here to the left."

Bumping into something in the dark, she cursed. "I think I found it."

"Take my hand."

"What?"

"Team members." Impatient, he held his arm out blindly. "Come on."

A second later, her small hand slipped into his.

They kept moving.

"Is it my imagination, or is it getting a bit lighter in here?"

"We must be getting close to the loading area. Keep going."

More shots.

"Do those fools not realize bullets ricochet off concrete?" he said again.

"Apparently not," Natalie answered, annoyance still evident in her voice.

"Why didn't they move in before?"

She shook her head, making him realize he could see her. "I held them off. But you barely showed up in time—I was running out of ammo. Did you bring more?"

"You should always be prepared."

She flipped him off. "That's why you're here. More ammo, another gun. The fact that you knew another way out is a bonus. Corbett did good, sending you." Tossing her head, she gave him a narrow-eyed, go-to-hell look. "You *do* have more ammo, don't you?"

He laughed, and saw her clench her teeth. A second later, he tossed her a couple of clips. Seething, she slammed one into her pistol. "Ready?"

He raised a brow. "For?"

"Moving out. Just in case the shooters have covered the back exit."

"You plan on blasting your way out of here?"

"Yep."

Once again she surprised him. The Natalie he'd known before would have wanted to stay hidden, hoping to pick them off one by one.

"Do you have any idea how many there are?" The cool, professional Sean was back. Astounded he might be, but he hadn't survived this long in such a dangerous game by letting his personal feelings get in the way of his job.

She matched her tone to his. "There are at least two out front. One east, one west. Both armed with AK-47s."

"Any idea who they are?"

"Does it matter? They want me dead. That's all I need to know. Now, how much farther?"

They both heard the shouts and the sound of boots running on cement toward them.

"We're over halfway there. Come on." He took off. This time, rather than following, she kept pace with him. Side by side.

Another round of gunfire, closer. Chunks of concrete spewed from the wall to the left of them.

Close. Too close. They both knew it.

"Damn it." Sean drew his weapon. "You go. I'll hold them off."

Ignoring him, she flicked off the safety and raised her gun. Leaning around the pillar, she aimed, waiting. An instant later, she squeezed off a shot.

Direct hit. The shooter's body jerked, then nose-dived forward. "Got him. One down, a few more to go."

He touched her arm. "They're shooting blind. No way can they see us back here. Come on." He took off.

She didn't waste time arguing.

Left, then right, then right again. With each turn, the darkness lightened.

"Here we are." Stopping, Sean pointed. "There's the loading area. See how that one metal door moves in the breeze?"

"Listen. The shooting's stopped. I wonder why?"

"Who cares?" He moved forward. "Let's get out of here."

She climbed onto the cement platform, staying

close to the wall. Sean followed right behind her.
When they reached the rusted metal door, she lifted
one side and pointed toward a narrow alley between two tall brick buildings. "That looks like
the only way out."

"No. Too constricted." Out of reflex, he grabbed
her arm. "We'd be sitting ducks. There has to be
another way."

Again, she jerked away. "Don't touch me."
Breathing hard, she glared at him, putting every
ounce of loathing she could into her expression.

Grimly, he looked around. He lifted his hand to
point and as he did, the remaining shooter fired off
another round, narrowly missing him. "Damn it."

"I don't think we have a choice." She jerked her
head toward the opening. "Are you ready to make
a run for it?"

He opened his mouth to respond, but a sound—
metal striking concrete—grabbed his attention. For
half a heartbeat, they both eyed the oblong metal
object rolling across the floor toward them.

"Time-delay grenade!" he shouted, grabbing her
and shoving her ahead of him. "Take cover!"

She needed no second urging. Sprinting for the
nearest concrete divider, she dove behind the wall
with him right on her heels.

The grenade exploded. Sean yanked Natalie into
his chest, ducking his own head. Fire flashed and
roared and the dilapidated building shook.

Dust and smoke and cement rained down on them.

Sean's mouth moved, but she couldn't hear for the ringing in her ears.

More gunfire. This, she could hear. The shooter— or shooters—were moving in, hoping the grenade had done the job.

Natalie looked at Sean. They didn't need sound to know what the other was thinking.

"One, two, three…go." Moving low and fast, they sprinted for the door. As they slipped through the unstable metal, bullets sliced into it where they'd been.

"Come on." They took off running, guns at the ready.

"Something's wrong." Natalie didn't like the way the pounding of their feet echoed off the alley walls.

"Too quiet."

Then, into the silence, they heard another sound. The unmistakable click of the grenade launcher firing.

"Down," Sean shouted, in the split second before the grenade hit to the left of them. It exploded on impact.

Natalie was thrown to the ground. Sean was lost somewhere in the smoke. *Damn it,* she thought as she struggled to stand up. It would be a crying shame for Sean to come back from the dead only to be killed on his first mission after. If anyone was going to kill him, it was going to be her.

At the exact instant she stood, squinting in the

smoke and fire and dust, head pounding, ears ringing, looking for Sean, the concrete wall above her came tumbling down.

Chapter 2

"Natalie?" Sean couldn't see. Couldn't hear. Couldn't breathe. He inhaled, struggling for air. Concrete dust filled his lungs, making him double over in a racking cough. He should be grateful—at least this proved he was still alive.

What about Natalie?

He called her again, his voice barely rising above a croak.

"Sean?"

Alive! Muttering a quick prayer to the powers that be, Sean attempted to push himself up. Though he tried to harness the energy of the relief that had flooded through him at the sound of her voice, he couldn't move. Blinded, disoriented and confused, he wasn't sure why.

"Sean?"

"Over here."

A volley of gunshots erupted. Those damned AK-47s, blasting a path toward them. Evidently, their pursuers had garnered reinforcements and were on their way to finish off what the grenades hadn't.

He cursed again, struggling to lift himself off the concrete.

"Sean, come on. We don't have much time." Natalie appeared out of the swirling cloud of dust, voice frantic. "Get up. We need to go. Now."

"I know." Struggling to push himself up, Sean frowned. He still couldn't move. Rubbing his eyes, he tried once more. No luck.

"What's wrong?"

"I can't—" Heart pumping overtime, he cursed when he saw the problem. The concrete wall had come down on his left foot, pinning him beneath it.

Funny how wounds don't hurt until you see them. True to form, the second he noticed, his foot began to throb.

"I'm trapped."

"Oh, God." Natalie's eyes widened, but she didn't waste time on small talk. "If I lift, can you try to wiggle out?"

He clenched his teeth. "No way you can lift this.

Even if you could, my foot's probably broken. I couldn't go far."

She shook her head. "No is not an option. I want you to try."

Team-leader words. He pondered this for half a second before giving her a cursory nod. "Go for it. If you can manage to lift the pillar, I can certainly manage to move."

Straining, she grabbed the concrete and gave it her best shot.

Nothing. Not even a minute bit of movement.

"Damn it all to hell."

Natalie continued to strain, pushing at the concrete.

"Stop," he ordered. "You need to go. Save yourself."

"I'm not leaving you." Her fierceness surprised him. Where was the timid mouse he remembered?

"You have to. If you stay, they'll kill us both."

"If I go, they'll kill you. That's not acceptable."

He put all his frustration into the look he gave her. "Listen to me—"

"No!" She threw herself against the concrete again. This time, he could swear the damn thing moved, even if only a fraction of an inch.

"Nat—"

"You've got to help me!" Eyes bright, she shoved again. Another infinitesimal movement.

Not enough.

"I can't."

"Do you want to die for real?" She shoved her face close to his, nose to nose. "Is that it?"

"No." He ground out the word, surprised to realize he spoke the truth. Even the dark secret he'd been carrying since before he'd met her wasn't enough to make him want to give up his life. Especially not since they were together again.

"Then help me!"

Pushing himself to a sitting position, he tried. Bracing his arms against the cement, he used every bit of his strength.

"Bingo."

The gunfire came again, louder. Closer.

"One more time," she urged. "You can do it."

"Rah, rah, rah," he muttered. Still, he was willing to try.

One more shove did the trick. Together, both their efforts succeeded in moving the concrete off his foot.

"Can you stand?"

"I don't know."

She held out her hand. "You have to. Come on."

Grimacing, he ignored her outstretched fingers and tried to get up on his own.

Though already swollen, it seemed his foot would support him. For now.

Standing, he tried to flash a triumphant smile but ruined the effect the moment he attempted to put weight on his injured foot. Staggering, he nearly fell.

With a loud sigh, she grabbed him. "We don't

have time for this." Arm around his waist, she half pushed, half lifted, and helped him back to his feet.

"Come on." Heading toward what had been the back of the alley, she helped him over chunks of cement, twisted metal and smoldering hot spots.

Dust choked him—them—but still she pushed on. He found himself admiring her determination.

"The explosion blew a hole in the backs of both neighboring buildings. The whole area could tumble down like a stack of cards. I'm hoping they don't know it yet."

Jaw clenched, Sean nodded. Sweat ran down his face and his foot hurt so badly he was half-afraid he might pass out.

Couldn't do that. Had to keep Natalie safe.

Or was it the other way around?

His field of vision narrowed, then went gray. Blinking furiously, he tried to keep his focus, fought to keep putting his uninjured foot in front of the other. He knew his wife's slender shoulders couldn't support his full weight.

The effort had him panting.

"Easy now." Nothing but cool satisfaction rang in her voice as she helped him over a large piece of concrete. She didn't, he noted sourly, even sound winded.

Away from the alley, the smoke-clouded air felt a fraction better. Cleaner. He tried to take a deep gulp and choked.

"Hurry," she whispered, trying to pull him forward. "We've got to move faster or they'll catch us."

He was doing the best he could, but she didn't need to know the extent of his weakness. Pushing himself, he struggled to lengthen his shaky stride and to keep from muttering curses each time he came down on his injured foot.

Natalie led him down a twisted alley, turning left then right and left again—so many different directions that he lost track of them. Finally, they arrived at the back of a pipe shop housed in an ancient stone building.

"In here. Auggie's one of my contacts. He's also a friend. He'll help us."

Her friend? Since when did contacts become friends? Allowing connections to become personal could be dangerous. That was one of the first things Corbett had taught Sean when he'd begun training many years ago. Natalie should know that—she'd had intensive training when she went to work with SIS.

Sean had actually opened his mouth to caution her when he realized he had no right. She didn't even consider him her husband anymore. After all, as far as she knew, he'd been dead for the last two years. By choice.

The back door was unlocked. Moving carefully, Natalie let herself in.

Sweating profusely, Sean leaned against the wall, drawing ragged breaths, trying to stay conscious.

"Are you coming?" she asked. If he detected a trace of impatience in her voice, it vanished when he raised his head and she got a good look at his face.

He must look even worse than he felt.

"God, Sean. You need a doctor." Slipping her arm around him once again, she helped him up the steps and into the back of the shop. Once he was inside, she closed and locked the door behind her.

"There. We should be safe for a bit."

A moment later, a bearded giant of a man came around the corner. He lifted one bushy brow when he saw Sean.

"Auggie!" Smiling, Natalie hugged him, her arm barely able to circle his neck. "This is Sean. He, uh, does the same line of work I do."

For some reason, the fact she didn't name him as her husband rankled.

"I'm her husband," he said, holding out his hand.

As Auggie's huge paw engulfed Sean's, Natalie crossed her arms. "He's not my husband," she told the giant man. Then, letting her gaze drift over to Sean, she gave him a hard look. "Not anymore, you're not. You're dead."

"Come on, Nat. I'm not dead." His protest sounded weak, he knew, but it was difficult to talk and still try to hold on to consciousness.

"You are to me," she said, turning her back and walking away.

"Sorry, boyo." Auggie clapped him on the back. Hard.

Sean winced. Looking about for a place to sit, he hobbled over to a large wooden crate. His vision grayed. Again, he clenched his teeth and rode out the pain and nausea.

With fumbling fingers, he managed to extract his cell phone from his pocket.

"No." Auggie snatched it out of Sean's hand. "Not unless Natalie says it's okay."

Dumbfounded, Sean could only stare.

"I heard my name." Natalie reentered the room. "What's up?"

"He was trying to call out." Tossing her the cell phone, Auggie gave Sean another baleful glare.

"Who are you calling, Sean?"

He could barely answer. "Corbett."

"Why?"

"I need to find a doctor."

"I know a good one." Natalie and Auggie exchanged a look. "Why bother Corbett? We don't work for him."

Vision wavering, Sean swallowed. At this point, if Auggie had announced he was a brain surgeon, Sean wouldn't have cared. "But I do—er, did. Let me call him."

"What's wrong with him?" Auggie spoke to Natalie as if Sean wasn't there.

"He hurt his foot. I don't think it's broken."

"Give. Me. The. Phone." Sean gritted out the words.

Without hesitation, Natalie tossed it to him. "Knock yourself out."

He punched in the speed-dial code. A second later, Corbett answered.

"I need the name of a doctor."

"What? Have you found Natalie?"

Sean answered in the affirmative, filling Corbett in on the details. He ended with his foot injury.

"Sean, ask Natalie. She'll probably have the best name. SIS has their own people and she's been working in that area the last two years."

While he'd been sequestered up in the Highlands, playing dead.

"Point taken." He sounded churlish, he knew. "At least give me a name."

"Very well." Corbett sighed. "Contact Dr. Pachla."

"Thanks." Sean ended the call and dropped the phone back into his pocket.

A half smile on her full lips, Natalie watched him. "Let me guess. He told you Dr. Pachla."

Reluctantly, Sean nodded. Even that slight movement brought him pain. "Can you contact him? Now?"

She looked at Auggie.

Smiling, Auggie nodded. "He's already on his way."

Sean leaned his head back against the wall. He

must have passed out, because the next thing he knew, he heard the sound of bells tinkling.

Natalie and the giant were standing close together, talking in voices too low for Sean to hear.

"Someone's here," Sean muttered. "Maybe the doctor."

"Or a customer. Just one moment," Auggie said, disappearing into the front of the shop.

When he returned a moment later, a tall, elegantly handsome blond man followed him. Something about him looked familiar, though Sean knew he hadn't met the man before.

When the doctor saw Natalie, his aristocratic features lit up. "Nat!"

"Dennie!" Natalie ran to him and hugged him. An intimate body hug with full frontal contact, Sean noticed, his irritation mounting.

For his part, Dennie didn't seem in any hurry to push her away.

"Ahem." Sean cleared his throat. "Over here."

Immediately, Natalie stepped away from the doctor. "Dennie," she said. "This is Sean. Can you take a look at his foot?"

"Of course." Kneeling beside Sean, Dennie held out his hand. "Dennie Pachla."

Sean shook it with as much heartiness as he could muster. "Sean McGregor."

Both of Dennie's blond eyebrows rose. "*The* Sean McGregor?"

Sean gave a weary nod.

Obviously surprised, Dennie glanced at Natalie. "But that would mean—"

"We were married." Natalie sounded grim. "Once."

"I was going to say that would mean you're not dead. But I guess 'we were married' works." Dennie continued. "You're not still?"

"Yes," Sean said.

"No," Natalie replied at the same time.

"We were never divorced." He glared at her.

"I'd think your death would have dissolved the marriage, don't you?" She glared back.

"Whoa." Dennie held up his hands. "Time out. I'll just be taking a look at this foot, and then I'll be on my way."

Auggie went up to Natalie and put his arm around her shoulders. "Why dinna you tell me he was back?"

She shrugged. "I just found out. You know I would have called you."

Sean winced. Though he'd always secretly harbored the fear their marriage wouldn't have survived his secret, watching her prove she'd made it without him hurt more than it should.

"We'll need an X-ray," Dennie said after a brief exam.

"No time," Sean responded.

A quick look at Sean's face showed Dennie he meant business.

"I'm thinking your fifth metatarsal might be

broken. Depending on how bad the break is, surgery is sometimes necessary."

"Not an option."

"A cast?" Dennie offered.

Sean shook his head no.

"Very well. I'll run back to my surgery and fetch a walking cast. It's a heavy boot," Dennie said as Sean started to protest. "You have to leave it on for six to eight weeks."

"Perfect." Sean held out his hand. "Thanks."

After a brief shake, Dennie rose and headed toward the door. Auggie followed. Only Natalie remained.

"What are you going to do?" she asked quietly. "After he puts that boot on your foot?"

"I came to protect you," he drawled. "So I'm thinking I'll accompany you back to London."

"London?" Though she never raised her voice, her anger simmered in her eyes. "I'm not going to London."

"That's the plan."

"According to whom?"

"Corbett. No doubt he's been talking to your father."

Briefly she closed her eyes. When she opened them, he saw determination and resignation in their depths. "I'm not going to London."

He sighed. "Fine. Then tell me, what are your plans?"

"You never answered." She crossed her arms and stared at him. Daring him to contradict her. "You first."

"I said I was going to protect you," Sean growled. "I'm going after him."

"Him?"

Though she shouldn't have had to ask, in a perverse way he was glad she had. He wanted to say the name of his enemy out loud. "The Hungarian."

"The crime lord?" She looked wary. "Why? Don't tell me Corbett's already given you a mission."

Sean had to remind himself that he had deliberately protected her from the truth about the Hungarian and the evil he could do. She believed his entire family had died in the same fiery crash that had supposedly killed him. In reality, they'd been slaughtered by the Hungarian's henchmen.

The man known as the Hungarian had completely destroyed both of their lives. The crime lord's vendetta was the reason Sean had pretended to die, so that Natalie's life might be spared.

And she knew none of this.

"No," he said slowly. "No mission. I'm not working for Corbett at the moment."

"Then why?"

"Because the Hungarian is after you."

He could see the stubborn light in her eyes. "The code I was working on before all this started was believed to be his, but what does that have to do with you?"

"That code may be part of the reason your team is dead, but he's after you because you're mine."

When she started to argue, he shushed her with a finger to her lips, oddly gratified when she didn't immediately jerk her head away.

"Natalie, I need to explain—"

"No." Violently shaking her head, she pushed herself away from him. "I'm not interested in your explanations. The past is over with. What's done is done. Save your story for someone who cares."

He ignored the stab of pain her sharp words brought, knowing that, at least in her mind, he deserved them. "What I have to tell you has a bearing on the situation now."

"I don't care. I'll be fine."

Exhaling, he dropped the subject, knowing he'd have to try again later. She had to know the facts so she'd know what kind of monster they were up against. "So will I."

"Have you ever worn one of those walking casts? You can't move the way you're used to."

"Concern? From Super-spy?"

"Don't call me that."

"Why not?"

"I don't like to be mocked."

"I'm not mocking you. Isn't that what you are now?"

"Look, you're out of practice, injured and you probably have no idea what's been going on in the underworld since you've been gone."

"Your point?"

"The Hungarian has taken out several of SIS's best agents. He may be responsible for what happened to my team. If you go after him alone, he'll kill you."

So much for faith in his abilities. If anyone needed protecting, it was she. Sean could take care of himself.

"I'm already dead, remember?" He gave her his best cold look. "If he kills me, I guarantee I'll take him down with me. Anyway, I'm not your problem anymore, now am I?"

Waiting with bated breath for her answer, Sean knew he longed for her to say the impossible. Extremely foolish, considering she'd been absolutely correct. Unless he killed the Hungarian, he didn't expect to come back except in a body bag.

Natalie opened her mouth to speak, then shook her head. "No."

His stomach clenched.

"You're absolutely right," she said, turning her back to him. "What you do isn't my concern. But I think you should know we're bound to cross paths sooner or later."

"What do you mean?"

One swift glance over her shoulder, the directness of her gaze taking his breath away. "If the Hungarian *is* trying to kill me, then I refuse to sit around and wait for him to come after me. I'm going to him."

Stunned, he could only stare. She'd just outlined his worst nightmare. "Why?"

She lifted her chin. "Among other things, I'm an SIS agent. My mission is clear."

Before he could comment, she spun on her heel and walked out of the room. A moment later, he could hear her laughter mingling with Auggie's.

Her life no longer included him. He should be used to the pain by now, but he wasn't. If anything, seeing her again, taking the brunt of her anger and knowing he deserved it had made him hurt even worse.

How the Hungarian would laugh if he knew. Despite Sean's sacrifices, the Hungarian had won a different sort of victory. Ironically, he'd succeeded in robbing Sean of the one person he'd loved the most. Natalie.

A few minutes later, Auggie returned alone.

Sean glanced up, then down at his hands.

"I'm worried about her," Auggie said, dropping onto the couch next to Sean.

"So am I."

"Are you?" The skepticism in the giant's voice had Sean raising his head. "You sure have a funny way of showing it."

Saying nothing, Sean gave the other man a look that plainly said *back off*.

Auggie ignored him. "If you want to go with her, all you have to do is make like you're weak, so she thinks you need her to protect you."

"I don't need anyone to protect me," Sean snarled. "Go away."

The other man didn't budge. "Swallow your pride, man. Just because you're a legend in the intelligence community doesn't mean you can't eat a little crow to protect the woman you love."

Wincing, Sean lifted his head. "Am I so obvious?"

Auggie chuckled. "Maybe not to her, but the way you feel is plain to see. Every time you look at her, it's like you found gold at the end of a rainbow. I can read you like a book."

"Wonderful," Sean groaned. "Her knowing how I feel is the last thing I need."

"Why? You're her husband."

"I was. Now, she hates me."

"Can you blame her?"

Silence was the only answer Sean needed to give.

"Look, if you faked your own death, it must have been for a good reason. I would think you can pretend to be an invalid to protect Natalie. What could it hurt, other than your pride?"

Reluctantly, Sean nodded. "Is she any good?"

Auggie's bushy brows flew. "I wouldn't know. You were the one married to her."

He felt his face color. "No, I didn't mean that. I meant is she any good as an agent?"

Chuckling at Sean's discomfort, Auggie shrugged. "She must be. She just got promoted to team leader, right before the tragedy with her team. I imagine she's finding that hard to live with."

As would anyone. But team leader? Sean couldn't wrap his mind around that. Though Natalie had changed, she'd always been more of a follower than a leader.

With a sigh, Auggie heaved his bulk to his feet. "Think about it, all right?"

"I will." Clumsily Sean stood, too, holding out his hand. After they shook, he met the giant's eyes. "Why are you doing this? You don't even know me."

"No, but I do know Natalie. I care about her. Nat needs all the help she can get. You know what the Hungarian is capable of."

Sean gave the other man a sharp look. "But does Natalie?"

"She lost her entire team."

Exhaling, Sean realized once again he'd need to swallow his pride and pretend to be something he was not.

But to save Natalie, he'd do anything. Even tell her the truth—that more of their marriage had been a lie than she knew.

Chapter 3

She'd forgotten his stubbornness. Sean was the only other person she knew who came close to being as obstinate as she.

In the past, they'd struck sparks off each other. Infuriating and exhilarating.

No longer.

Now, being around him made her insides knot.

The bright sunshine and cloudless autumn sky felt at odds with the turmoil inside her. If the weather were a reflection of her mood, there'd be booming cracks of thunder, lightning sparking among swirling clouds and rain pouring down in sideways sheets.

She refused to let the cheerful day pull her from her black mood.

Red wig and sunglasses firmly in place, Natalie power-walked down the boulevard. Past the bakery, where the mouthwatering scent of freshly made bread made her pause, and past the coffee shop, where strong coffee with a dollop of cream waited.

The October air felt brisk, which she welcomed. Cool air and exercise. Good for the body and the mind. Little by little, she felt her tension ease. She rolled her shoulders, stood in the warm sun and breathed deeply.

When she'd regained her calm detachment, she headed back, managing to smile and nod at other shoppers.

Entering Auggie's store from the front, she greeted Auggie as though she was only a customer and didn't know him. He responded in kind, asking her if there was anything he could help her find.

This oft-used code told her they were not alone. She couldn't go into the back yet to say her good-byes to Sean.

Goodbyes? She huffed, pretending to look at an assortment of candy. He didn't deserve a goodbye, not really, not after what he'd done.

But this was Sean and she'd loved him for so long. She couldn't help but feel as though the heavens had given her an added blessing, allowing her to hear his voice one more time.

If she were honest, something inside her, some small, foolish part, wanted to see his beautiful face one last time. To drown in the warmth of his eyes, touch his skin, breathe his scent. She craved this in much the same way she'd craved sex right after they'd married.

She'd given up sex. Certainly, she should be able to give up Sean. After all, she'd done so once already, two years ago. She'd gone on with her life and, while she couldn't unequivocally say she was happy, she'd survived without him.

Sean. The love of her life. The one man she'd trusted. To learn he'd betrayed her hurt almost as much as his death.

Yet she couldn't make herself walk away. Not without knowing why he'd done what he did. She should demand answers; hell, she *deserved* answers.

But did she really want to know? Could she really handle the truth, whatever that might be?

As she strolled nonchalantly around the small shop, she realized two things. One, though she'd never been a coward, she didn't yet want to know the why of his defection. Someday, maybe. But not just yet.

And two, she couldn't leave him. Not now, not until he was healed. And if some tiny, foolish part of her whispered *never,* she ignored it.

Finally, the other customer left. Auggie came to her and touched her arm. "Come on."

Sean sat slumped over on the cot, his head down. He looked up when they entered, then looked away.

Natalie crossed the room silently and dropped down beside him. She motioned Auggie to leave, which he did.

Once the other man was gone, Sean raised his head, but still wouldn't look at her. "You're going," he said. His voice sounded hollow.

Her throat ached. Wrapping her arms around herself, Natalie came to a decision. "No. I'm not leaving. I need your help," she said softly. He met her gaze then, his own full of frustration and stubbornness and physical pain.

Swallowing, he dipped his chin. "I think maybe it's the other way around." He dragged a hand through his unruly hair. "I'm the one who needs help." The soft gravel in his voice told her how much of an effort it cost him to say the words.

Despite herself, her heart melted. For sanity's sake, she kept her expression stern. "I'm serious."

"So am I."

"Help you go after the Hungarian? If so, I'm in. I want the bastard." Now she had his attention. "I do think he's responsible for what happened to my team. There are rumors that he's running a major arms-smuggling operation. The code we were working on could be about that."

He gave her a startled look. "Do you have any proof?"

"Not yet. But we figured out a rudimentary character-exchange system. Signal for phrases, that sort of thing. There was one section no one could crack. I'd planned to take a shot at it. Then my entire team was cut down in cold blood."

"How?"

"Murdered at their desks."

"At SIS? With full security on duty?"

"We worked a lot of nights on rotation. Someone disarmed the alarm and took out two of the guards. Everyone in the office that night died."

"Except you?"

"I wasn't there."

"And the code?"

After a moment's hesitation, she nodded. "All traces gone. Except for the copy I'd taken with me."

"Do you still have it?"

"Yes."

He swore. "I want that son of a—" Taking a deep breath, he met her gaze. "I want him, you want him and Corbett has offered to help. Don't you think we have a better chance of taking him down if we work together than if we work separately?"

"Maybe." She didn't dare let her guarded hope show. "Are you proposing we work as a team? If so, then like I said a moment ago, I'm in."

He looked down at his leg. "Are you sure?" he asked, quietly. "Before we do this, we both need to be one-hundred-percent certain."

Even after two years apart, she realized he knew her too well, knew that she was offering this as a way to protect him.

"Please," she added, because she didn't know what else to say.

As he opened his mouth to speak, his cell phone rang.

Watching while he answered, again she was struck by his sheer masculine beauty. Her heart hurt.

How she'd missed him.

And, she thought bitterly, how she hated him for what he'd put her through.

"Here." He handed her the phone. "It's Corbett. He wants to talk with you."

Gingerly, she took the phone and said hello.

"Your father's worried about you," Corbett said, by way of greeting. "Why haven't you contacted him?"

Guilt made her wince. This was the first time in her entire career she'd had to ask her father, a former Lazlo operative, for help.

"You sent Sean," she volleyed back. "You knew he wasn't dead." She couldn't believe it. Corbett had known Sean was alive. As a family friend, Corbett had attended the funeral, offered his condolences, watched her suffer when with two simple words—*he's alive*—he could have alleviated her agony.

But he'd never said them.

Then, when she'd been in the worst trouble of her

career, she'd called her father and Corbett had sent Sean back to her. As if she wanted him back.

A horrible thought struck her. Had her father known, too? Had he withheld the truth, even as he comforted his grieving daughter?

The depths of such a betrayal would be impossible to fathom. Such a thing would rank right up there with her mother abandoning her when Natalie was six.

"I sent the best, per Phillip's instructions." Corbett's clipped voice told her the subject wasn't open for discussion. "Sean got you out, didn't he?"

Clenching her teeth to keep from saying things she might regret later, she took a deep breath. "Is that all you wanted?"

Silence. Stalemate.

"I need your help," Corbett finally said. "I've got a code for you to crack." Since the Lazlo Group had their own team of code specialists, this request meant the situation was tense.

As if he sensed this, Sean made a restless movement, dragging his hand through his thick, dark hair.

Damn, she wanted him.

Tearing her gaze away from Sean, Natalie swallowed.

"Hello?" Corbett's tone grew even grimmer. "Are you there?"

"Yes. Sorry." Taking a deep breath, Natalie forced herself to loosen her death grip on the phone.

"Will you take a look at the code?"

She sighed. "I'll try. But, I've got another code to figure out as well."

"Another code?"

"Yes. My team and I were working on it when…" She choked, unable to finish the sentence. Clearing her throat, she continued. "I'm sure my father told you."

"He did, but not that you still have any of it."

"I do."

"Excellent." He sounded impressed. "I have a feeling you'll see similarities with the one I'm sending."

That got her attention. "Seriously? Where'd you get it and where was it going?"

"One of my operatives intercepted it from a dead man. We think the missive was headed to the Hungarian."

What remained unspoken resonated over the line. This code might be the key to unlocking the secret of the Hungarian's identity and location. She and her team had been so close. Too close. Instead of them bringing their enemy down, he'd attacked and eliminated them.

"How quickly can you get it to me?"

"I'm working on that as we speak. Once you have it, how quickly can you crack it?"

She eyed Sean, who'd crossed his arms and appeared to be trying to follow the one-sided conversation. "I don't even have a computer."

"I'll get you a laptop."

"Fantastic. But make it ultralight. The last thing I need to be dragging around is a seven-pound computer."

"Of course. The Lazlo Group always uses the latest technology." Corbett sounded distant. "I didn't plan on sending you a dinosaur."

"Good." Distracted now, her fingers itched to get started. "It will be interesting to see if your code and the one I have are the same."

"We have a short time frame."

"You're telling me. It's difficult enough trying to stay alive and keep Sean from getting killed. Trying to crack a code takes intense concentration. I don't have that luxury now."

"Sean can help you with that. You can rely on him to get you the space and quiet you need."

Rely on him? She almost laughed at the irony. "I'll figure out something."

There was a muffled sound, then her father's voice came on the line. "Are you all right, baby girl?"

"Papa?" She rubbed her now-aching temple. "Corbett didn't tell me you were in Paris." Paris was the home base of the Lazlo Group.

His deep chuckle didn't mask the concern in his voice. "I was worried."

She had to ask, had to know the truth. "Did you know Sean wasn't—"

"Not now." The stern tone of her father's voice

was tempered by love. "We'll talk about this later, once you and Sean have worked everything out."

She bit her lip. "We won't—"

"Natalie, you have no choice. Not now. Maybe once all this is over, but not until then."

He was right, damn it. She sucked in her breath. "All right, I'll do my best."

"That's my girl." Her father chuckled again, making her wish she could hug him. "Now, here's Corbett."

"How soon can you be ready to do a pickup?"

"Of the code?"

"Of course." Corbett didn't even pause, and she realized he'd known immediately that she wouldn't be able to resist such a challenge. Though he had his own code specialist, Natalie had gained a reputation as the best. For good reason. She used to brag there wasn't a code she couldn't crack.

Super-spy, Sean had called her. When it came to breaking tough codes, he hadn't been too far off the mark.

"Where and how?"

"You'll need to meet one of my agents." Corbett named a location, an old abbey on the other side of Glasgow, maybe an hour away at the most. "Can you be there at 1600 hours?"

Auggie came back into the room, looking at Natalie for permission. She nodded and, returning her gaze to Sean, glanced at her watch. "That gives us two and a half hours. We have to rent a car and…yes. We'll meet your man at 1600 hours."

With that, she handed the phone back to Sean. She had nothing further to say to the man she'd once trusted. She'd decipher his code, because more than anything she wanted the Hungarian taken down. After that, they were through. As through as she was with her once-dead husband.

Understanding without her telling him anything, Auggie moved closer and squeezed her shoulder with his big hand. Grateful, she reached up and covered his hand with hers. Over the past year, they'd become good friends. Auggie, like Dr. Pachla, had hinted he was willing to become more, though she'd been careful not to encourage any closer relationship.

Sean had been the love of her life. Her marriage to him had ruined her for any other man.

As she closed his cell phone, Sean met her gaze, his own sable eyes clear. Though she knew he'd heard her tell Corbett about the stolen CD, he didn't mention it. "We'll need a car."

Auggie removed his hand from Natalie's shoulder. "There's a car-rental agency a few miles from here. I can drive you," Auggie offered.

"Excellent." Sean nodded. "I have a new identity." He gave Natalie another long look. "Corbett created it for me after I 'died.'"

She kept her face expressionless. "What name?"

"Roark McKee."

Another pang stabbed her heart. Roark had been the name they'd planned to call their son, whenever she conceived.

"Can you drive?" Natalie regarded his walking cast with skepticism.

"It's my other foot, luv." The familiar endearment seemed to slip casually from his lips. She stiffened, unwilling to comment, to let him know how much he had hurt her.

"Fine. You rent the car. No one is looking for you."

When they reached the car-rental agency, Natalie waited in the car with Auggie while Sean went in.

"Take it easy, lass." Auggie spoke in a soft voice, his burr becoming more pronounced. "You still love him, don't you?"

Miserable, Natalie stared at the spot where Sean had disappeared inside the doors. "I don't know how I feel anymore. Aug, I should just hate him for what he put me through."

"But you can't?"

Her halfhearted shrug was the best she could do. Her throat was too clogged with emotion to allow her to speak.

"You're a damn fine operative, Natalie Major. You've moved on with your life. Don't let this get you down."

"You talk as if his returning from the dead is a small thing."

"I'd say that depends on your perspective."

She crossed her arms. "There's no excuse for what he did."

Auggie shrugged. "Maybe. Maybe not. You won't know for sure until you talk to him and find out why."

"I'd rather forget him." Even as she said the words, she knew she was lying. Already, even when separated from Sean by a matter of minutes, she craved him.

A horn honked. "There he is." Auggie pointed. "He's gotten a nice Mini, now hasn't he?"

Though she'd seen the tiny cars out and about, Natalie had never wanted to ride in one. They were too small, for one thing, and Natalie was a tall woman. She couldn't imagine her six-foot-three inch husband crammed into one.

This would make the term *close quarters* no exaggeration.

Both Auggie and she exited his car at the same time, walking over to the Mini. Auggie circled the blue vehicle, a gleam of admiration in his eyes.

Sean rolled down the driver's-side window. "Best I could do," he said, before she could even comment. "We didn't have reservations and they're a bit low on cars."

Auggie chuckled as he walked up beside her. "One thing about it, no one will suspect you're a spy in this tin can."

Natalie glared at him.

"You'd better get in," Sean said, not smiling. "Before someone recognizes you."

He was right, damn it. She gave Auggie a quick hug, then yanked open the passenger door and wedged herself into the seat.

"See, it's not so bad." Reassuring? Sean? She wondered what else had changed about him in the two years he'd been dead.

He handed her a well-creased map, then started to pull away from the curb. "I've marked the location of the abbey where we're to meet Corbett's man."

Not sure how she felt about his automatic assumption that he would be leader, she opened her mouth to dispute him.

The back window shattered.

"What the—?"

"Get down," Sean yanked the wheel to the right, heading into a narrow alley between buildings. "Someone's shooting at us."

She was already down, head on her knees, or as best as she could in the tiny car. "They must have identified me."

"How?"

"I don't know."

He took another sharp turn and they shot out into the street. Horns blared and a lorry narrowly missed smashing into their side.

"We're going to have to ditch this car."

"Not now. We've got to meet our contact in—" she glanced at her watch "—forty-five minutes."

"I don't care. If they keep shooting, we'll have no choice."

"Yes, we will." Natalie sat up straight, smoothing down her hair. "You're not in charge here, you know."

The narrow-eyed look he shot her would have lit a cigarette. "Don't start this. Not now."

After a moment of surprise, Natalie threw back her head and laughed. "We already sound like an old married couple, bickering."

"We are an old married couple." His expression softened. "Last month was our sixth anniversary."

"Would have been," she corrected, her chest aching. "If you hadn't died."

The tightening of his jaw was his only response.

As they entered downtown Glasgow, traffic increased.

They were sitting ducks at a complete stop, especially if a shooter had a high-powered rifle.

But no gunshots shattered any windows, and they reached the other side of town without incident.

"Too weird," Natalie said.

"I agree. There's no reason why they'd simply give up. Unless…"

"They knew where we're going."

"Impossible."

Natalie shook her head. "Is it? You and I both know better."

"So we'll be extra careful." The tight set of his mouth told her he wasn't happy with the situation.

"Get in, meet Corbett's man, grab the code, and get out."

When they arrived at the abbey, the parking lot was curiously devoid of the normal crowd of tourists' vehicles. Only one other car had been parked in one of the marked spaces.

"They're closed on Thursday," Sean told her. He chose a spot on the other side of the lot, as far from the lone car as he could get.

Natalie understood his reasoning. One never knew where a car bomb might be planted.

Silent, they got out of the car.

The weather had changed and a light mist still fell, shrouding the air in a blanket of damp. The slate-colored sky exactly matched the weathered stone of the ancient building. As abbeys went, this particular one wasn't much to look at. Part of the exterior had crumbled, and it was more of a ruin now than an actual building.

But the sense of age…

Natalie wasn't a mystical-minded person, not in the slightest. But the energy of this place, the eerie invocation of timeless power, made her hesitate. She felt as though she were actually intruding, as though her very practical feet should not tread on this hallowed ground.

If Sean sensed the same, he gave no sign.

Keeping close to the crumbling wall, they moved toward the old cemetery on the hill. They were to meet their contact near an ancient crypt hidden behind several immense oaks.

A tingle on her left hand had her glancing down. The wedding ring Sean had given her—the woven band of silver she'd never taken off or switched to her right hand as widows were supposed to do—had grown hot. The ring was old; it had once belonged to Sean's grandmother. Sean had always called the Celtic design "fairy metal." He'd teased Natalie, telling her his grandmother claimed to have found the ring in an enchanted circle, left for her by her fey lover.

The way it responded to this place, Natalie could actually believe the story.

"You never took it off." Sean's quiet voice, raspy with pain, broke into her musings.

"No." For a sharp instant, she was glad the sight of her wedding ring had hurt him. He had no idea how much she'd suffered, believing him dead. Or how much she continued to suffer, now that she knew the truth.

But then, he apparently had never realized how much she'd loved him.

He'd stopped moving forward. Though he still hugged the wall, he watched her, waiting for her to tell him more.

Instead of answering, she brushed past him, taking the lead.

The open space between the end of the building

and the beginning of the cemetery would be where they were most exposed. Crouching low, Natalie ran. After a muffled curse, Sean followed, awkward in his heavy cast.

Several large trees by the wrought-iron gate provided a shelter of sorts. Natalie slipped behind one and Sean took another. Though there was no breeze, the gate was open, as if their contact had left it so when he'd passed there before them.

"Ready?" Low-voiced, Sean stood poised to move.

With a jerky nod, Natalie answered. She'd let him take the lead again—for now. At least this way she could cover his back if need be.

The old stone crypt was in the farthest corner of the ancient graveyard. They kept as close as they could to the larger monuments and statues, using them as granite shields.

When they were halfway across the cemetery, the crypt exploded.

Chapter 4

Natalie jumped on Sean, pushing him to the ground.

"Stay down," she growled.

Though he narrowed his eyes, he did as she asked. In the past, he'd led and she'd always followed. No more. Still, with his muscular body pinned beneath her, she was suddenly hyperconscious of their positions.

Thoughts like that in times like this would get them both killed.

"Come on." She yanked his arm. "We've got to get out of here."

"Get off me so I can move." His voice sounded

strangled. Whether from arousal or from annoyance that she'd taken the lead, she couldn't tell.

She scooted down the length of him, purely for revenge, then got to her knees. "We'd better stay low. Come on."

Making sure he was following her, she crawled to the nearest section of iron fence. "Corbett's man is dead."

"We'll mourn him later." He paused, catching his breath. "I'm thinking he took the code with him."

"Lost in the explosion, no doubt. But they'll check to make sure." She glanced over her shoulder. "We're going to make a run for the car."

"Right." His tone was dry.

Too late, she remembered his walking cast. "Can you do it with that thing on?"

"Yes." Again, her assuming the leadership position seemed to bother him. But, unlike the Sean she'd once known, this Sean clenched his jaw and said nothing else.

She didn't have time to reflect on what that meant. "You go first."

He shot her a go-to-hell look. "Why?"

"In case you can't get over the fence on your own. I can help you."

Without another word he got to his feet and hobbled to the next statue. At this rate, they'd be there all day.

Somehow, Sean managed to climb over the fence

unassisted and without getting shot. Natalie could only hope their luck would hold.

In the meantime, she needed to take steps to make sure she wasn't recognized again.

When they reached the car, she went to the passenger side. She'd let him drive. She'd learned a long time ago how to pick her battles.

Natalie kept a sharp lookout for any hint they might be being followed, but not a single car made the same turns.

"Are they playing with us?" she wondered out loud.

"Could be. They have to know their rigged explosion was a failure. We're not dead. Maybe they *want* us alive."

"For what reason?"

"The code. Could it be possible that damn code is more important than any of us realizes?" Intent on the road, his expression gave away none of his thoughts.

"Surely they know their own code." She heaved a sigh, wishing she could still rest her head on his shoulder as she'd done in the old days.

"Unless it's not theirs."

Natalie stared. "What do you mean?"

"Think about it. Why would the Hungarian be so eager to get some old, coded message away from you? Whatever information it contained, he could simply change."

"But if it belonged to someone else—"

"Like one of his enemies."

"Who would be foolish enough to go up against someone so powerful?"

Sean smiled wryly. "The Hungarian has a lot of enemies. Maybe a bunch of them got together to plan something."

"Wouldn't we know? I mean, both SIS and the Lazlo Group have undercover operatives in place. We would have heard something by now."

But they both knew that wasn't necessarily true. Huge secrets had been kept before, men killed, wars fought, with no one in the intelligence community the wiser until it was all over.

This time, when their gazes met, for the space of a heartbeat, she couldn't look away.

Taking a deep breath, she bit back questions she didn't want answers to and instead pointed out a sign on the corner ahead, advertising a discount drugstore.

"I need to stop at that store."

Sean shot her a look that plainly said he thought she'd lost it. "I know you like to shop, but your timing sucks."

She nearly smiled. Nearly. "Trust me, this is a necessity. But it doesn't have to be that one," she said as they drove past. "Any chemist's shop will be fine."

A quick stop at the first druggist on the way out of town, and she had what she needed. Climbing back into the midget-size car, she buckled up and dropped her small bag on the floor. "I'm good."

The stark expression on Sean's face made her catch her breath. "What's wrong? What happened?"

"I just got off the phone with Corbett. He already knew he'd lost a man."

Natalie bowed her head. In the undercover community, the death of a fellow operative was treated the same way it was by firefighters and policemen when one of their own died—with respect and sorrow.

"Did you convey to him my condolences?"

"Yes. He was on his way to talk to the family."

She winced. "That's one duty I wouldn't want."

"No one would. But as head of the agency, Corbett takes his responsibilities seriously."

As if she didn't know. Her own father couldn't speak highly enough of the man. When her father had lost his legs in an explosion while working undercover, Corbett had helped him find the best surgeons, paid for a wheelchair and paid to renovate his home, even knowing he'd have to retire. The two men still talked regularly. Their stories about the life of a secret agent were why she'd gotten into the business in the first place, though in her bid for some sort of independence, she'd chosen to work for the government rather than the Lazlo Group.

"I'm assuming Corbett had his own copy of the code."

"Of course. He's working on another way to get it to us, along with a computer."

She nodded. "Perfect."

"Yeah. But still, we need some help. What about your resources? Can you access any of them?"

She stared. "Resources? You mean like SIS?"

"Exactly."

"No." She hoped the single word would shut him down. "I'm on leave. Administrative, due to the trauma of losing my entire team. As far as they know, I'm recuperating on the French Riviera."

She waited for his questions, but apparently he had none. The sky had grown darker and it wouldn't be long before the inky night became complete. Suddenly exhausted, she yawned.

Noticing that in the dim light from the dashboard, Sean smiled. Again, she felt the beauty of that smile like a punch in the stomach. "Stop it," she said crossly. "It's been a long day."

"We'll find a place to stop for the night."

"Great."

Parking in the back drive of the first B and B they came to, Sean went inside and secured them a room. When he emerged, he looked grim.

"I rented one room."

"Why?"

"Security reasons."

Too tired to argue, Natalie simply nodded.

Opening her door for her, he helped her out. Natalie allowed this, telling herself his touch didn't feel good, not at all. The shiver that ran down her spine was due to the chilly air, nothing more.

"Wait." She dug into her knapsack and retrieved the bandana Auggie had given her. This she placed over her head, tying it under her chin. "Camou-flage," she said. "Best I can do at the moment."

Sean raised a brow but didn't comment.

They walked into the brightly lit sitting room, neither of them speaking, staring straight ahead. The tension between them seemed palpable—almost unbearable, like the electricity in the air right before a thunderstorm. Natalie had to grit her teeth to keep herself pleasantly smiling.

Their hostess, a plump, bespectacled woman with a shock of bright orange hair, led them to the rear of the house. "You two even have your own bath," she exclaimed. "All of the rooms upstairs have to share the big one at the end of the hall."

Once they reached the room, she handed them a folded paper listing breakfast options and left them alone.

Natalie eyed the double bed with dismay. "I'm guessing she didn't have a room with a king? Or even a queen-size bed?"

"I'm sorry," Sean said, sounding anything but. "I can sleep in the chair if you'd like."

Eyeing his walking cast, Natalie tried not to think about how badly she wanted to touch him, to run her hands over his once-beloved skin while breathing in his never-forgotten scent, to feel him move inside her again. "I'll sleep in the chair. Since you're driving, you'll need your rest more than I."

He narrowed his eyes. Once, he'd been able to read her thoughts, her desires. Or at least it had seemed that way to her. Once. No longer.

They'd been so happy. Or, she amended, *she* had. Obviously, Sean had felt differently. She'd never understand how he could do such a thing to the woman he supposedly loved.

"I'll sleep in the chair," she repeated, in case he wanted to argue. "But first, I need your help with this." Opening the paper bag from the drugstore, she removed her purchases. "I'm going to cut and color my hair."

For a moment, he froze, reminding her how he loved her hair, short or long. After lovemaking he'd always run his fingers through it.

Ruthlessly, she shut down the memories. "I know it's short, but I've got to make it shorter. I can't be recognized again. It's compromising our mission."

A trained spy, Sean understood. She could tell from the set of his chin that he didn't like it, but he knew the reasons why changing her appearance was necessary.

The way he studied her sent shivers down her spine. Finally, he nodded. "Unfortunately, you're right. What do I need to do?"

"Let me wet my head in the lavatory sink." As

soon as she'd accomplished that, she combed through her already short locks and returned to the bedroom. "Now I'm ready."

"I'm not." He didn't sound as if he were joking.

Ignoring him, she dug out her newly purchased scissors, holding them out, along with the comb. "Will you do the honors? I could do the sides, but I'm afraid I'd make a hopeless mess of the back."

Accepting the scissors, he moved the desk chair over by the bed. "Sit here in front of me."

One deep breath for strength, and she did as he asked. The mattress springs creaked as he took a seat on the bed directly behind her. "How short?"

Did his voice tremble?

"Chin length." Her hair touched her collarbone now, which meant he'd be removing two to three inches.

As he combed through her hair, she sighed and closed her eyes. When they'd first met, he'd loved her long hair, insisting on brushing it every night. Sometimes those sessions had turned heated, and they'd made fierce and passionate love. Her entire body warmed just thinking of it.

She could tell from the catch in Sean's breathing that he hadn't forgotten either.

The first time he skimmed the comb through her hair, a chill skittered along her spine. How she wanted to turn her head and press a kiss into the palm of his hand, the way she used to. Instead she held herself perfectly still, trying to relax.

Impossible.

His breath tickled her ear, her throat. Any moment now… She braced herself for his whisper-soft kiss, so familiar she ached for it, so alien she dreaded it.

When it never came, she reminded herself to breathe. Too much time and deception had passed between them. They each had a job to do, for their country, their agencies and their own personal satisfaction.

Giving in to old memories, old lusts, would accomplish nothing.

"It's done." His voice sounded husky. When he ruffled her newly shorn locks, she couldn't suppress a shiver.

To keep from doing something foolish, she jumped to her feet and went to the mirror over the desk.

She looked…different. The choppy haircut brought out the hollows of her high cheekbones, but it was more than that. Life had returned to her face. Her eyes were no longer a muddy brown, but the amber color they'd once been, the color Sean had always teased her about by saying they glowed with passion.

Passion. No matter how she might try to hide this, even from herself, passion burned in her and her body knew. Each moment she spent with Sean, hearing his voice, longing to feel his touch, marked her.

Natalie was no longer Natalie Major, the efficient

Super-spy, the woman made of ice. Despite her best intentions, she resembled Natalie McGregor, the woman hopelessly in love with her mate.

From behind her, Sean made a strangled sound. In the mirror, she saw him standing on the other side of the bed. His dark eyes glowed, full of such heat she nearly gasped. Their gazes locked and held.

Slowly, she turned, her pulse beating erratically.

When he came to her, gathering her in his arms, the scent of him, the feel of his muscular body against her, was almost unbearably painful.

Still, she hungered.

His touch as intimate as the old days, he trailed his hands over her skin and caressed the small of her back.

Ah…this. Arching against him, she lifted her face for his kiss, starving. He met her halfway, crushing her mouth beneath his. His lips devoured hers, demanding, hard and punishing, making her whimper a weak protest at first. But as he deepened the kiss, she welcomed his mouth as though two years had been erased.

Finally, her world was…full.

Stupid. With a hiss, she jerked away. Though she immediately felt bereft, she hid it with a scowl. "Don't do that."

The lazy look he gave her had amusement mingled with the desire. "You're mine," he stated, with all the confidence of a lion surveying his pride.

"Not anymore."

"Always." His voice dared her to disagree.

Though she could have argued, Natalie chose not to dispute his words. He'd always been able to tell when she was lying.

Instead, she grabbed his head and pulled his mouth down for another kiss. Impatient now, anger blazing into desire and need, grief becoming longing and the shame of his betrayal subjugated into want, she used her tongue the way he'd always found unbearably arousing, stroking the inside of his mouth, suckling his tongue. Reckless, abandoned, she tore at his clothing, craving him naked, hard and deep inside her.

His breathing came harsh, unsteady.

"Natalie?"

"Don't talk," she growled. "Not now."

Grabbing her hands to hold them still, he held her away. The question she saw in his eyes felt like a dash of ice water down her back.

What had she almost done?

"I—" Hand to mouth, she backed away, as far as the small room would allow. Still, her body throbbed, wanting him.

"Shhh," he told her, not coming after her. Was that grief she saw flash across his rugged face, or merely thwarted desire? No matter.

He'd saved her. She owed him that. She'd nearly made another huge mistake to add to her already huge list of them.

Even now, trying to clear her head, one look at the front of him, at his blatant arousal, and she nearly said to hell with it and went to him.

Closing her eyes, she drew one ragged breath, then another. How well she remembered the fit of him, tightly sheathed inside her. Their lovemaking had been explosive, intense and fulfilling, something she'd known no other man could measure up to.

"I'm sorry," she told him, absurdly on the verge of tears.

"I understand," he said, though she knew he didn't. Aching, she wanted to weep.

"I'm…" She couldn't find the words, though she knew she should be asking questions. Ask, hell, anyone else would demand an explanation. As if anything he could say would explain his betrayal.

When her mother had left, Natalie was six, but she well remembered her questions, and the way her father had had no answers. Finally, he'd told her she was better off not knowing.

Now she understood what he'd meant. Sometimes knowing the truth could hurt more than whatever the mind could imagine. She'd been an adolescent when she'd finally figured out her mother hadn't wanted her, didn't love her, and had left of her own free will. Up until that point, Natalie had convinced herself the woman had been abducted, forcibly dragged away from the daughter she adored and the husband she loved.

No longer a child, nor a teen with easily bruised emotions, Natalie knew she should demand answers. Should, but wouldn't. She didn't really want to know.

Instead, she brushed past Sean, grabbed the box of hair coloring off the table and went into the toilet, closing and locking the door behind her. She needed to walk, needed it the way a smoker craves a cigarette. A breath of fresh air and a brisk, two- or three-mile walk would clear her head and help her regain her shredded composure.

The crack of gunfire woke him.

Sean jerked up, years of training enabling him to snap instantly awake. Since he was still fully clothed, including his damned uncomfortable cast, he shoved himself to his feet and did a quick survey of the room.

Natalie was missing.

Moving as fast as the boot would allow, he grabbed his gun and yanked open the door, then moved down the hall to the front door. He opened it and cautiously stepped onto the porch, closing the door behind him.

Another round of gunfire had him dropping to the ground.

Where the hell was Natalie? Combined with the streetlights, the full moon provided ample light, but he couldn't see her anywhere. Maybe she'd taken cover. Maybe she wasn't there. So where the hell was she?

He had to assume she was safe so he could concentrate on taking out the shooter.

Keeping close to the brick building, he moved in the direction of the gunshots. He heard sirens, which meant someone had called the police. This could be good—or bad. It might stop the shooter, but there was no way he or Natalie could talk to local law enforcement.

The shooting stopped—Sean could only guess the gunman had heard the sirens, too, and was calculating how long he had before he needed to escape.

More confident now, Sean moved closer. He'd fitted his Glock with a silencer, which would do the job nicely if he had to take out an enemy. Though he'd rather capture the guy and question him. With the police on their way, that might not be possible.

Right now what mattered was keeping Natalie safe.

Rounding the corner, Sean stopped. A long, open stretch lay between his building and the next. No way was he going out there blind, making himself a perfect target.

The wail of the sirens grew louder.

A shadow moved.

Sean raised his gun.

Natalie jumped up and began running toward him.

His heart stopped.

Then, knowing he had no choice, he jumped out into the open, both to cover her and, he hoped, distract the shooter.

When she reached him, she knocked him back around the side of the building. "What do you think you're doing?"

"Shhh." Listening for more shots, he heard only the rapidly approaching sirens. "He's gone. We've got to get back to our room."

Though her gaze shot daggers, she didn't argue. Together, they ran, keeping close to the wall.

Another shadow.

"Get down," he shouted, just before the shooter again opened fire.

She dropped like a rock. Sean felt a searing heat right above his cast. "Damn it," he cursed.

Rat-ta-tat-tat. And again. The sirens were closer still. Again the shooting stopped.

"What's wrong?" Natalie asked, her eyes and gun trained in the direction of the gunman.

"I'm hit."

"Where?"

"The leg."

Natalie was beside him. "Cover me." Then she was tearing her shirt to make a tourniquet on his leg. A rapidly spreading crimson stain showed the wound right above his walking cast, as he'd suspected.

"You're determined to lose that leg, aren't

you?" she muttered. "Come on. We've got to get out of here."

"Can't." Perspiration ran from his forehead into his eyes.

She muttered a string of curse words strong enough to make a sailor blush.

"What the hell were you doing out here anyway?" he asked.

"I needed a walk," she growled, her expression daring him to say anything.

"A walk." He stared, wondering if he'd ever really known her. The Natalie he'd known and loved wouldn't have left him to go for a walk.

"We've got to go. Now." She grabbed his arm.

"No." He jerked away. "I'll do it on my own. You're not strong enough."

"Been there, done that. I got you out from under a ton of concrete, didn't I?"

"Blind luck."

Another round of gunfire. More smoke. He swore.

Who was this psycho? They didn't know and had no time to find out. Again he cursed his clumsiness.

"Blind luck, my ass. Try blind skill." This time, when she grabbed him, he didn't resist. Half tugging, half shoving, she got him moved to the limited shelter provided by a Dumpster trash bin. His eyes drifted closed. Shaking his head, he tried to keep them open. "Let's go."

"Stay conscious. Sean, you've got to stay with me."

"Why?"

The question appeared to blindside her. "Because," she told him fiercely. "This isn't the way you want to go out."

"True. But it's taking all I have to stay conscious. So tell me, Super-spy. Now what?"

"Usually I have backup or radios or one of a hundred tricks a well-equipped spy has at her disposal." She snorted. "I'm guessing there's no use looking toward the sky for a James Bond-style helicopter to magically appear and rescue us, right?"

The fact that she could joke in such a tense situation made him attempt a smile. "Let's move."

They made it to the next building without incident, huddling under the small portico over a back door, protected a bit by metal trash cans.

"Listen," Sean said. They both heard the sharp click as the shooter reloaded. Any second now, he'd squeeze off another volley of shots.

Heart in his throat, Sean tensed. He'd been away from this game far too long.

"Is he following us?" Natalie whispered.

"You broke protocol," Sean suddenly told her, fiercely. "I thought you were a professional."

"I am. I—"

"Professionals don't leave without telling their partner. You could have gotten us both killed."

"Stop, Sean." She glared at him. "I screwed up,

true. I'm sorry. But this shooter was obviously heading for our B and B. I surprised him out in the open, before he was ready. He could have cut us down in our sleep. So part of this worked out for the good."

Attempting a nod, he sucked in his breath instead. He didn't know how much farther he could go. His strength ebbed out of him with every breath.

"How—" He couldn't finish.

"How did he find us? I don't know. Maybe we need to do a sweep for bugs."

Another series of shots. Several rounds cut a wide swath through the metal trash bins.

"Too close. Run," he gasped. "Go. Save yourself."

"No." She prodded him forward.

Assess. The. Situation. She wouldn't leave him. Nor he her, he knew. Never. His life wouldn't be worth living if he lost her again. Result. He had to save himself, and, in doing so, save her.

The sirens were nearly upon them. Somehow, he had to get them to safety. No way could they attempt to explain to local authorities what had happened here.

"Come on." He made his voice harsh. Strong. Commanding. "Let me lean on you."

Without hesitation, she moved her shoulder under his arm. Taking a deep breath, he lurched forward.

Chapter 5

Somehow they made it out from the porch and across the alley, moving through the neighboring yards, backtracking to their B and B.

The tourniquet held and he left no trail of blood to betray them.

Leaning on her heavily, Sean forced himself to shuffle his feet, step after step after painful, labored step. Grunting from the strain, Natalie kept her shoulder under him, staggering at times in her attempt to keep them moving.

Luckily, their room had French doors that led out to a small terrace. Privacy was always a good thing.

"Get me in that way. We need to avoid any questions from our hostess."

"My thoughts exactly," she huffed.

Shouts from the porch they'd recently vacated told them the police had arrived. Sweat rolling down his brow, Sean struggled futilely to increase his pace.

"Come on," she urged. Together they shuffled forward as fast as they could. Sean kept his teeth clenched against the pain, forcing himself to move without uttering a sound of complaint.

Finally, they slipped through the metal garden gate. Natalie pulled it closed behind them, then quickly picked the lock on the French doors.

Pushing Sean inside, she slammed the door closed and drew the curtain shut. He staggered to the bed and dropped down on the mattress, breathing heavily.

They were safe. For the time being.

"What now?" he panted.

Licking her lips, she swallowed. "I have to see about getting that bullet out of your leg." She rummaged around in the knapsack she'd carried with her all day, finally pulling out a small box. Then she grabbed the pillowcase off one of the pillows and tore it into strips, and some of the strips into pieces.

"No way." He tried to rise, but couldn't. Fighting against nausea and unconsciousness, he couldn't even lift his leg to move it. "Damn thing burns like hell."

"Hold still." Her voice, still harsh and sounding completely unlike her, stopped him cold.

Through a haze of pain, he eyed her. "Like I can move," he ground out, wondering if she'd ever been shot. He had, almost more times than he could count, though never seriously. No major organs or arteries. This was one aspect of his job he hadn't missed over the last two years.

"You might be wanting to move in a minute." Was that a warning? Without waiting for his response, she pushed him back and began unwrapping the makeshift tourniquet that had kept him from bleeding to death.

Each pass of the material hurt like hell.

Gritting his teeth, he bit back a few choice curse words. Instead, he managed to keep his voice relatively level. "What do you think you're doing?"

"I've got to get the bullet out. And it'll be painful."

Her matter-of-fact tone told him she was cutting him no slack. Still, he'd done fieldwork for too long to argue with truth.

"How about whiskey? Do you have any?"

She barely even glanced at him. "No, of course not. Do you?"

He shook his head, wincing as a piece of fabric caught on the edge of his raw wound. The sharp bite of pain made everything spin, and he sucked in air, trying to stay conscious.

Wouldn't do to show weakness before the woman he was supposed to protect. He bit back a groan.

"I'll be as gentle as possible." Was that a hint of

concern in her voice? She began rummaging in the plastic box.

"I appreciate that," he managed, the pain overwhelming. Worse, she hadn't even started searching for the bullet. "Let's get this over with." He grabbed a piece of cloth from the small stack she had in front of her, twisted it and shoved it in his mouth.

"Wait a second." She continued rummaging. "I think I saw some pain pills in here. Aha!" She held up a small, brown plastic bottle. "These might work."

He took two and swallowed them dry.

"Ready?"

He nodded.

She gave him a sympathetic smile. "Go ahead and pass out if that will help."

Pass out? Who did she think he was? "Hell no," he growled, mumbling around the cloth. Finally, he yanked it out and glared at her. "I've had bullets removed in the field before. I want to make sure you do this right."

In the act of disinfecting her hands with waterless cleanser, she paused. "I'm sure I can handle it."

"Have you ever done this before?"

"No."

At least she was honest. Still, her answer didn't give him the confidence in her ability he'd hoped for.

"Have you?" she asked.

He jerked his chin in a brief nod. "Of course.

Make sure you sterilize whatever you use to get the bullet out."

Intent on separating the rest of the blood-soaked material from his skin, she didn't respond. When she had the area clear, she sucked in her breath with an audible hiss.

The sound had him raising his head. "Are *you* gonna be okay doing this?"

Instead of answering, she bent over him and, setting her jaw in that intent way she had, picked up a pair of tweezers, coated them with waterless cleanser and held a match to them. "Sterilized," she said, still focused on the bloody mess the bullet had made of his leg.

An instant later she began poking with her tweezers.

Shoving his temporary gag back in place, Sean felt as if she was stabbing him with a fiery torch. Damn, that hurt. He tried to force himself to breathe deeply and evenly, fighting to maintain consciousness.

Struggling not to cry out, he broke out in a sweat. Hot and cold, dizziness and nausea, then, despite his best intentions, everything faded to gray and he passed out.

By the time she located the bullet, Natalie's shirt clung to her back, drenched in perspiration. She dropped the bloody piece of metal onto the plastic lid and picked up her small bottle of rubbing alcohol. One thing she'd learned early on in her career—when doing fieldwork, always have a rudimentary first aid kit handy. Luckily, she hadn't lost hers in the gun battle.

Bracing herself, she dumped half the bottle into Sean's open wound.

"Aaaah!" Sitting bolt upright, Sean cursed. Then, mercifully for both of them, his eyes glazed over and he went back to unconsciousness.

"Good," she muttered. Snatching up a needle and thread, she lit another match and sterilized the needle. Then, praying Sean stayed unaware, she began stitching up the wound.

Later, with the wound dressed and wrapped, Natalie made herself a cup of tea with the tiny electric kettle the B and B provided. Taking a seat in the chair at the side of the bed, she watched her husband sleep, wishing she could sort out her chaotic emotions.

Previously an optimist, she'd learned the hard way that clouds didn't always have silver linings. People died, friends lost touch, and previously warm and sunny days were prone to become gray with a simple change in the direction of the wind.

Life wasn't fair and if you didn't like that, there wasn't a damn thing you could do about it.

Her rose-colored glasses forever broken, she'd grieved heavily over the loss of Sean. Her friends and coworkers had worried about her, finally contacting her father to help them pull her out of the deep, dark depression.

And she'd realized she had to go on without Sean. Somehow. Burying the ever-present sorrow deep inside her, she'd set about redefining her life, vowing she would live on her own terms now.

Though she'd always enjoyed her job, she hadn't become fiercely intent on it until after Sean died. She'd made SIS her entire focus.

This showed in her work. In the two years she'd lived alone, she'd been promoted twice. Headquarters had even offered her a desk job, a plum most agents would have snatched eagerly.

Not her. She'd refused, preferring fieldwork. Every new assignment had brought her a fierce kind of happiness—the only happiness she knew these days. She lived for the excitement, the adrenaline rush. After all, danger and her emerging talent for cracking codes had been a working distraction from her pain.

She'd solved a few solid cases, one of them huge. Her father had been proud of her and Corbett Lazlo had even offered her a job working for him at the elite Lazlo Group. She'd said no, her loyalty to SIS strong. Her anger at Lazlo for the role he'd played in her life was still there, even if she knew it was unreasonable. Then her entire team had been killed and she'd become a target. And once again, the fates had intervened. Emerging from the grave, Sean had reappeared to claim her. Not dead. Not even hurt.

All along, she'd been living a lie. Her entire life—before and after his so-called death—had been false.

The turmoil this knowledge caused her felt overwhelming.

She had no time to deal with it. The mysterious and evil Hungarian they hunted seemed involved with it all—the SIS, the Lazlo Group, destroying her life and her team—and Sean's, too, if she were honest.

Sean's voice startled her.

"Could I have some water?" He licked his lips, his dark gaze as powerful as always.

Nodding, she rose and went to the tap, half filling a glass and carrying it to him. She moved the other pillow behind him and helped him sit up before handing him the glass.

He drank eagerly, gulping so quickly he spilled most of the water on the sheets. When he'd finished, she took it from him and placed it on the nightstand.

"You're going to be all right," she said.

Though he nodded, something in his gaze as he searched her face made her feel as if he knew what she'd been thinking. Hell, maybe he did. They'd used to joke about being able to read each other's minds.

She'd once found this immensely satisfying, proof they were totally compatible. Now, she found it unsettling.

"What?" she asked, hating the defensive tone to her voice.

"Do you want to explain to me why you felt the need to go for a walk in the middle of the night, endangering our mission and our lives?"

A flash of anger warred with guilt. "Only when you feel like explaining to me how your entire family and you died in the same accident. In a car you weren't even supposed to be in. And since you haven't mentioned them, I'm going to assume your family really is dead." She knew her voice was laced with pain and anger, and chose to focus on the anger. "I've long known someone had to be responsible, though no one—not Corbett, not my superiors at SIS—claimed to know who. You know, don't you?"

For the space of two heartbeats, he simply stared. Finally, he gave a slow nod. "I do."

Though she was skirting the edge and moving closer to dangerous territory, she realized she wanted to know, at least this. "Tell me."

He breathed a sigh. "The Hungarian."

"That's what I thought. Especially when you said he might be after me because of you. Why?"

When he looked away, the stab of grief felt fierce.

"It's a long story," he said. "And while you might be ready to hear it, I'm not sure I can tell it."

"Don't you think it's time I knew the truth?"

Dragging a hand through his hair, he looked

down, up, anywhere but directly at her. "Yes. But you deserve to know everything, all at once, and what I've done might make you hate me even worse."

About to tell him she could never hate him, she bit back the words. Her chest ached. "After all this, you're still hiding something from me?"

"No more than you're hiding from me."

"Quit trying to change the subject." She shook her head. "I'm not hiding anything. This isn't about me, it's about you."

His smile mocked her. "See? You can't go on feeling responsible and guilty."

"Easy for you to say. My entire team died. I didn't. I've got to figure out what the hell I know that the Hungarian wants to keep silent or that he wants to discover."

"Natalie, listen to me. You need to stop feeling responsible and trying to fix this. It might not all be you."

She stared at him, heart in her throat.

"Some of what's happened—hell, *most* of what's happened—might be because of me."

"You keep saying that. But I don't understand. Tell me."

Though he looked reluctant, this time he held her gaze. That was Sean, never one to back down from bad news. "They might have gotten word that I wasn't really dead. The Hungarian knows if that were true, you would be the one person who could bring me back to life."

"The Hungarian used me to get to you? That makes no sense."

"You asked about my accident, my family's *accident?* There was no car crash, no accident."

Bewildered, she put her hand to her throat. "If you're telling the truth, there was one hell of a massive cover-up. Even SIS has the car crash in their files."

"No car. No crash."

Briefly, she closed her eyes. "Why? Why would anyone go to such lengths?"

"To protect you from the Hungarian. He's sworn a vendetta on me."

The old-fashioned word seemed out of place, wrong. "A vendetta?"

"Blood feud. That's why he slaughtered my family."

"Slaughtered?" Closing her mouth, she squared her shoulders. "Is that what really happened, Sean? Your mother, father, sister—he killed them? All of them?"

"Yes." He inhaled, the sound loud in the quiet room. "He murdered my entire family for revenge."

"Why? Because of Kitya Renkiewicz, his mistress?"

He shook his head. "I killed Kitya, but I had no choice. If I hadn't shot her when I did, she would have killed me. But the Hungarian didn't give a rat's ass about her. My problems with him started long before Kitya."

"That doesn't explain why you faked your own death."

"You were next. The only way I could stop him from coming after you was for him to believe I was dead."

"You couldn't come to me, tell me what was going on? Instead, you engineered a massive cover-up and faked your own death?"

He nodded.

In disbelief, she stared. Her pain felt ten times stronger faced with the unbelievable extent of his lies.

"*This* is all you can come up with?" She wanted to hit him. "I was your wife, the one person you could trust. You let me believe you were dead, ripped my heart out, and *this* is your explanation? Sean, I grieved for *two years*. Your *death*," she spat the word, "changed my life."

"It changed mine, too."

She wanted to weep. "It's the most ridiculous thing I've ever—"

"It worked."

"No. It didn't. You're here now. I'm getting shot at. Nothing worked." Raising her gaze to his, she let him see the depths of her bitterness.

"Nat, I—"

"No." She lifted her hand, managed a careless wave. "I don't want to talk about this anymore."

"You don't understand."

"Ah, but I do." The rancor seeped through to

her voice, and she let it. "That's why you need to drop it, Sean."

"But—"

"If you want to work with me, don't say another word."

Turning her back, she blinked back tears. Their marriage had seemed so different, so *real*. Based on mutual respect and trust and love, or so she'd believed.

That only proved what a gullible fool she'd been.

No more.

"Go to sleep, Sean." Without waiting for an answer, she got up, turned off the light and sat in the chair by the window.

"What about you?" His voice, combined with the room's darkness, made her ache again.

"I'm going to sit here awhile." She kept her tone curt. "I've got a lot to think about."

Sean dreamed. For the past two years, he'd been unable to forget Natalie's kiss. Or the feel of her body, supple and welcoming, wrapped around him while they made love.

Now, in his dream, he kissed her again, with all the ferocious passion pent up inside.

Instead of kissing him back, in his dream she froze, her huge amber eyes wide open.

He tried to deepen the kiss.

She made a sound of denial against his mouth.

Stunned, he backed away. What the hell was this?

He knew she was angry with him. He didn't blame her. But he'd been certain her fury would melt the instant his mouth touched hers. Always, always, always, the touch of his lips had made Natalie melt.

Not this time.

Made of ice, she hadn't softened as he moved his mouth over hers. Hell, she hadn't even parted her lips.

Had she really gotten over him so completely?

In his dream, sorrow engulfed him as he realized she had.

Worse, she didn't understand why he'd done what he did. If she couldn't handle that, how would she deal with the rest of his past?

He'd given her up to save her life. During the two years away from her, he'd almost managed to convince himself that he had no regrets.

He'd been lying.

The intensity of his pain woke him. Fully awake, he punched his pillow.

"Does your leg hurt?" Natalie's voice, from across the room.

"Like hell." Nearly as much as his heart. He pushed himself to a sitting position and clicked on the lamp, looking for her.

With her legs curled under her, she occupied the room's single armchair. He couldn't help but remember how she used to sit, head tilted just so, lost in the pages of a good book. This time, she'd been sitting in the dark, as lost in her thoughts as he'd been in his dream.

"Are you okay?"

"I'm fine." Blinking, she stared at him. The hostility in her voice dropped the temperature in the room ten degrees.

"You're in no condition to go after anyone. I'm going to ask Corbett to get you out."

He tried to move, to push himself out of the bed, but couldn't make his leg go anywhere. "Don't even think about it."

"Sean, I'm perfectly capable of taking the Hungarian down alone. As it is now, you've become more of a liability than an asset."

Stung, he bit back a sharp retort. "You're using my leg as an excuse."

Her reply was short and sweet. "Sorry. Sue me."

He couldn't believe the sweet irony of their situation. "Look. You can't just dump me. You wanted to tag along with me to protect me, and the entire reason I wanted you nearby was to protect *you*." He laughed, a tired, bitter sound, even to his own ears. "Admit it. And I'm not done protecting you yet."

"I don't need your protection."

"Nor I yours." He wished he could kiss her, hard and quick, like he had in the old days.

But he couldn't, so he wouldn't.

"How about a truce?" Her quiet question surprised him.

"I didn't know we were at war."

She shook her head, her short spiky hair making her look as if she'd just climbed from his bed. She was almost unbearably sexy.

Damn and double damn.

Swallowing, he collected his thoughts and tried again. "Look, we both want the same thing, right?"

She nodded. "I want to find him."

"And learn who he is and why he—"

"Did what he did."

"Yes."

He held out his hand, bracing himself for the cool slide of her fingers into his.

"Let's work together."

"We've already tried that." She didn't take his hand. "You're wounded. You need to go home. Once you're healed, you can rejoin me."

"I doubt you'd be alive."

The statement didn't appear to faze her.

"Such confidence you have in me," she drawled. "Why don't you let me worry about that, and you go back to doing what you do best—protecting your own ass."

The barbs were getting sharper. He elected to opt out rather than continue slinging words.

"You know me. A little thing like this leg won't get me down. We make a good team, Nat. Always have, always will."

"Our marriage is over."

He swallowed. Though she hadn't meant it to be, that sentence was the most hurtful of all. "I'm not talking about our marriage. We are a working team, colleagues. You know that neither of us can get to the Hungarian alone. And to try to do so is suicide. Quit being so stubborn and admit it. Before you get yourself killed."

Tilting her head, she considered his words, forced by their vehemence to put aside her personal feelings. "You may be right."

"You know I am."

Ignoring this, she continued. "If we're going to be a real team, we need to lay down some ground rules."

This should be interesting. "Like?"

"I'm in charge." She said it so smoothly he wasn't certain he'd heard correctly.

"Uh, no."

She cocked her head, crossed her arms, and merely looked at him.

Still sexy as hell. But ten times more infuriating.

"Natalie, sweetheart—"

"I'm not your sweetheart."

He tried again. "I've been doing this sort of thing far longer. I'm a trained assassin, for pity's sake. I'm older, stronger and male."

"So? Men lead and women follow, is that it?"

Since she had it pretty much in a nutshell, he didn't see the need to elaborate. "You've got it."

He waited for the explosion.

Instead, she threw back her head and laughed.

It was a truly amused, gut-rolling, belly-shaking laugh. The sort of laugh a confident woman had, a woman who knew what she was and where she was going.

Natalie had never, in the entire time he'd known her, laughed like that.

He stared at the beautiful woman who'd been his wife and finally acknowledged the truth. She'd become a stranger. Two years had passed, an eternity of living separately, time enough for both of them to change.

Though he might long for things to be as they'd been, too much water under the bridge ensured that could never happen.

Yet he couldn't stop wanting her.

Despite the desire coiled in his gut, Sean had to sleep. Though his restless mind and tumbling thoughts tried to pump him full of adrenaline, his exhaustion was so complete that he found himself nodding off in the middle of Natalie's next question.

"What?" he repeated, groggy and slow and wishing he could simply wrap himself around her and drift off to sleep.

"Get in the bed," she repeated. "You look like you might pass out at any moment."

Grateful, he crawled for the pillow, barely registering her touch as she tugged the blanket over him.

Outside, the rain beat steady and heavy, drowning out the noise of the traffic and the city. Sean's last thought as he drifted off to sleep was how he'd give anything to wake up with Natalie warm and willing in his arms.

Chapter 6

"Sean, I need the truth."

He started, yanked up out of a light doze. The soft question came out of nowhere, the dark room amplifying the sensual sound of her breathing, of her silky voice. "I gave you the truth." Blinking, he cleared his throat. "Honestly, I told you what really happened."

"No. You told me pieces." Her tone made it clear she thought there was more. "You left part of the puzzle out. The biggest piece. What's the real reason the Hungarian wants to destroy you?"

His heart thudding dully in his chest, he swallowed. She'd asked the one question he'd dreaded for so many years. The one question that, if he answered, might completely and utterly destroy whatever speck of love remained in her heart for him.

Propped into the corner of the high-backed chair, her elegant neck looking impossibly long, her short, copper-colored hair sticking up in wanton disarray and her half-lidded amber gaze appearing sultry, she made him want her all over again.

He couldn't help but wonder if she knew her beauty struck him dumb. Fervently, he hoped she didn't.

While he stared, she stared back. Finally, she narrowed her eyes, the dim light from the lamp making them appear to glow golden. "Are you even awake enough to talk?"

He could have taken the coward's way out—told her he wanted to go back to sleep and they'd talk about this in the morning. But he was tired of running, tired of hiding. And, even though he'd given her a partial truth, he was damn sick and tired of having her think he'd disappeared because he didn't care.

"I'm waking up." Sean couldn't help but wonder if she remembered the way he always woke around her—aroused and ready. She used to love teasing him, until they both were panting and breathless.

Damn. Remembering didn't help his current situation at all. Pushing himself up, he plumped up the pillow and propped it against the headboard. He was careful to keep the blankets piled on top of his lap.

"At the time, I believed I had no choice." It was

the closest he could bring himself to admit he might have, in the awful grief and rage, made an error in judgment.

"I thought our marriage was based upon trust. Love. Respect. You've proved me wrong with your lies. You weren't the man I thought you were, Sean." Her voice broke. "The man I loved."

He opened his mouth, closed it and swallowed. In this, with secret upon secret upon secret, he wasn't even certain where to begin. There were some things he'd believed he would never have to tell her.

Now, he knew he had no choice. If they were ever to have a second chance together, Natalie had to know everything.

She misread his hesitation as refusal. "Cut the crap. Tell me everything."

Everything. He closed his eyes and sighed. The rest of what he had to tell her tasted like bile, though he knew someday she'd have to know the truth.

All of the truth, no matter how much it hurt.

"Start at the beginning, so I can keep this straight." Her clothes rustled as she moved. "Begin with the family reunion."

Though his feud with the Hungarian went back much further than that, the family reunion was a good place to start. Natalie had been scheduled to arrive close to the same time as his parents. A missed flight had saved her life.

Clearing his throat, he began. "What the Hungarian did to my family earned him a special niche in hell.

"I arrived on the island early, planning to surprise my folks and you. I'll never forget jumping out of the rented boat and jogging toward the main house, full of excitement.

"The pool of blood on the front porch was my first clue something was wrong."

He tasted bile and swallowed, forcing himself to continue. "Bloody footprints in the foyer had me running for the den. My family was there—or what was left of them. The killers had dragged them into the center of the room and tossed them in a horrible, bloody heap."

Eyes wide, she watched him. "Dead?"

"Oh yes. They were all dead. Brutally murdered. Missing limbs, or eyes or heads. From the expression on their faces, they'd suffered horribly before they died."

The blood leached from her face. "I'm so sorry."

Ignoring her, he continued. "Frantic, my first thought was for you, my wife. I couldn't find you. Your body wasn't in the bloody carnage of all that remained of my family. I searched every inch of that doomed vacation house. Nothing. Nada. Zip.

"As if losing my parents and brother and sister weren't enough." Again he swallowed, blinking back tears. "I couldn't bear losing the woman I loved more than life itself, too. But I couldn't find you."

"I wasn't there," she reminded him, softly.

Ignoring her, he went on. "For one terrible moment, I believed you'd been taken hostage by him, a man who had no problem ordering the brutal torture and slaying of innocent people. But when I turned on my cell phone to call the police, I found the message you'd left while I was in flight. I played it back. Your cheerful voice seemed out of place as I stood in the middle of the bloodstained room and played it, again and again and again."

"The message I left telling you my flight had been cancelled." Her whisper was hoarse, the pain in her voice as raw as his own.

"Yes." He didn't tell her that right then he'd fallen on his knees and thanked God she was alive. Natalie was alive. As long as she lived, the Hungarian hadn't won. She'd been spared the sight of the carnage, of the message written in blood on the living room floor.

This is only the beginning. We're not done.

He'd known then. The Hungarian had done this to make him pay.

The blame for all these deaths could be laid squarely at his feet. The murders were his fault. Repercussions always had a way of catching up with you. He should have known that.

But even then, even grieving and hurting and furious, he'd tried to figure out a way to save Natalie. Because he'd known the Hungarian wouldn't rest until she'd died a horribly slow death, just to punish him. Sean had wanted to spare her that fate. So he'd died instead.

Now, once again, he faced the consequences of his actions. Proving no one ever got off scot-free.

"Sean?" Her voice brought him back from the horrific memories. "Why didn't you contact me, tell me what was going on?"

"I couldn't risk it. If anything had happened to you…"

"I'm a trained SIS agent." She sounded impatient. "I can protect myself."

"I wasn't thinking clearly. I'd just lost my entire family." It was the first time he'd admitted it, even to himself.

He cleared his throat. "Nat, if I hadn't died, the Hungarian would have killed you. You wouldn't have seen it coming. Then he would have put a price on my head."

"What did you do to make him hate you so much?"

Ah, the six-million-dollar question.

He took a deep breath, both dreading what he had to say, and relieved that he could finally say it, struggling to find the right words. Awash in pain he hadn't allowed himself to feel in twenty-four months, two weeks and three days, he knew he couldn't break down in front of her. Not now, when every word he said could impact his future.

Their future, if he dared to dream of such a thing.

"Years ago, before I met you…" Despite his resolve, he choked up.

Restless, he almost got up from the bed. But she hadn't moved from her chair. Who knew—maybe all that psychology crap was right and allowing her to be in a seated position, and thus dominant, while he reclined on the bed, would make her feel better. And maybe, just maybe, help her understand. There was so much more he needed to say.

Yet once again, the words stuck in his throat.

The tears shimmering in her eyes nearly undid him. "It's really awful, isn't it?" she whispered.

He nodded, the truth catching in his throat, choking him. The most horrible lie of all.

But before he could think about how or even whether to begin, she got up and sat beside him. She placed her hand on his arm, sending shock waves through him. For a moment he simply existed, breathing her scent, feeling her touch, and felt he'd finally been allowed a glimpse of heaven.

"I—" he tried to begin.

Her voice as soft as her touch, she asked, "Instead of going into hiding, why didn't you go after him and kill him? Make him pay for what he's done? You were—are—an assassin. Some say the best. If anyone could bring the Hungarian down, it would be you. How could you allow a bastard like that to live?"

Wincing, he looked away. "That's the same question that's haunted many sleepless nights." His insides churned. "I wanted to. God, how I wanted to. But I knew it would take time to find him. Your life was at stake. I couldn't keep you with me always, and I couldn't use you as bait—too much risk. Yes, I wanted him to pay, but I wanted you to live more. I made a snap decision, dazed by grief, full of rage."

"So you faked your death."

Put that way, his choice sounded cowardly. In truth, leaving her, making her a widow, had been the most difficult thing he'd ever done. Bar none.

"I had no choice."

She shook her head. The grief in her expressive eyes mirrored that in his heart. "That's where you're wrong. You did, Sean. You did. I would have helped you hunt him down and kill him. Back then, we made a hell of a better team than we do now."

Shoulders shaking, she got up and walked away, to the only place she could go, the small lavatory, leaving the rest of what he had to tell her trapped on his tongue.

Staring after her, he wondered if she'd ever understand. Or if she'd ever forgive.

And she didn't even know the worst of it.

It took half an hour, but Natalie was reasonably certain she'd managed to hide all signs of her bout of weeping. Except for the red eyes, and she was banking on the dim lighting to hide that.

She'd halfheartedly hoped Sean had fallen asleep while she'd hidden in the bathroom, but when she opened the door he still waited, sitting on the edge of the bed with his head in his hands.

Despite herself, her best intentions flew out the window. "Are you all right?"

"Fine." Straightening, he looked away. "Remember, there's more I've got to tell you."

The bed dipped as she sat down beside him. "You can do that later. I think I've had enough for one day."

"But—"

"Seriously. Unless what you want to tell me will endanger my life if I don't learn it, let it be for one more day. I can't take any more today, okay?"

Finally, he nodded. The stark relief that flashed across his handsome face was painful to see. Especially since she felt the same—as if she'd dodged a bullet.

"Then let's talk about something else."

"What?"

"Anything," she said. "You choose."

"Tell me why you're here, hiding from your own agency. Why you called Corbett and not SIS for help."

"My entire team was slaughtered in SIS headquarters. Cut down in cold blood, without warning. Since SIS was breached once, I have no doubt it could be breached again. I don't trust anyone there at the moment."

"Breached?"

"We had a mole. Roland Millaflora. You might have heard of him."

"But he was captured, right?"

"Yes. But I don't know who he was working for, or worse, if he had help inside. So I've cut myself off from headquarters. As far as they know, I'm on the French Riviera."

She yawned, then stood up and started to move away. "Let's get some sleep. I have a feeling we're going to need it."

"Not yet." His gaze darkened. "Come here, Nat."

She opened her mouth and closed it. "Why?"

"Just come here."

Suspicion had her frozen before she remembered he was a wounded man. Moving to his side, she reached for the water glass to refill it. "Do you want more water?"

He grabbed her arm, tugging her toward the bed. "No. I want you."

Shocked, she stumbled and nearly fell. Righting herself, she perched on the edge of the bed, empty water glass still in hand. "You're…you're hurt, in pain."

"So distract me." Waiting, he watched her. "Come here."

Trying to pretend the husky timbre of his voice didn't affect her, she shook her head. If she moved, even one-tenth of an inch, she'd be all over him. Devouring him, as she'd wanted to do ever since he'd come back from the dead.

Not good.

Mouth dry, she tried to concentrate on something else. Like how badly she needed to file her nails. Or brush her hair. Except she couldn't. Such a routine grooming shouldn't become sensual, but with Sean in the room, even breathing aroused her.

So she kept still, unwilling to move and let him know how he affected her.

"Stop." Pleased with her brisk tone, she shook her finger at him. "It's almost morning. You need to try to rest. Thinking about sex won't help you go to sleep."

"I haven't been with anyone else."

Her heart skipped a beat. "What?"

"You heard me."

Why he felt compelled to share this information, she didn't know. Unless he thought telling her would make her give in. She was glad he didn't know how badly she wanted to give in. She supposed she ought to consider herself lucky he was injured.

"Your faithfulness—or lack of—doesn't matter."

"Yes, it does." He sounded firm. "I took a vow, in a church. I swore before God and this green earth that there'd be only you."

Impatient now, afraid to think about what his confession meant, she shifted on the bed. "You don't have to lie. I know you. You're a very sensual man. There's no way you went so long without any…feminine attention."

He didn't answer, drawing her gaze to him as he'd no doubt known his silence would.

Despite the hell he'd just gone through, he looked damn good. The devil himself couldn't have looked better. His rugged features had gone serious, watching her in that intense way he had, his eyes dark and full of secrets. His black hair gleamed in the artificial light, one lock falling forward onto his brow. In times past, she'd always brushed that wayward strand back, and he'd grabbed her wrist and kissed her hand.

She shivered, telling herself to look away yet totally unable to.

Sean.

He waited, powerful arms relaxed, his hands dark against the pale blanket, and let her look at him. No doubt, she thought with irritation, he wanted her to remember the sensual pleasures they'd once shared. He wanted to tempt her with more than an apple, even knowing that if she touched him now, she'd be giving up what was left of her soul.

She couldn't, wouldn't let that happen. No matter how badly she wanted him, this dark, fallen angel who'd once belonged to her.

The woman who'd loved him had died when she'd thought he'd died. Just because he'd come back to life didn't mean she could.

"Two years, Sean. It's been two years. You pretended to be dead, for heaven's sake! Don't you dare try to seduce me now."

"Natalie, I—"

"No." She shifted uncomfortably. "And you shouldn't even be thinking that way. You're wounded."

"Only my leg and foot. The rest of me is fine."

His quip elicited no smile from her. "Stop."

"Please," he said. That one word nearly undid her, because the Sean McGregor she'd known had never had to ask her for anything. She'd given of herself freely and with pleasure, always happy to put her love for him in physical terms.

"You're killing me," she managed, clearing her throat to try to force out coherent words. "Quit. Just quit."

Another man might have laughed or attempted to defend himself by pointing out that he'd done nothing, made no move.

Not Sean. He understood, as she'd known he would. Their relationship had always been both cerebral and physical.

Her sigh was full of regret. "Working with you is more difficult than I thought it would be."

"You're telling me." He gave her a rueful smile, finally letting her see the pain in his eyes. "I'd leave, but moving would be rather painful right now, in more ways than one."

Closing her eyes, she inhaled sharply, unable to

prevent herself from remembering what he'd been like when fully aroused.

"I'll go." She pushed herself to her feet, moving unsteadily toward the bathroom.

Closing the door, she turned on the tap and splashed water on her face. Cold water. Eyeing her dripping face in the mirror, she hated the lingering desire she saw there. She'd had two years to lose every hint of weakness inside her. Evidently she hadn't been successful. One look from Sean had her wanting to melt.

Taking a deep breath, she emerged from the lavatory.

Sean had fallen asleep. Good.

Without changing her clothes, she climbed into the bed next to him, sliding under the covers. They both needed their rest. Tomorrow promised to be a long day.

Tonight promised to be an even longer night.

The chime of her cell phone woke her. Groggy, she flipped open the casing and muttered a hello.

"Natalie?" Not only did her father sound wide awake, but unnaturally cheery. "Are you all right?"

"Yes." She shot Sean a quick glance. The phone and her voice had awakened him, too. He lay on his side and watched her, eyes gleaming in the dim light. "We were still asleep. Late night."

"Did you learn anything relevant?"

"Only that someone really wants me dead. Some shooter with an AK-47 came after me. Sean was hit."

The sharp sound of her father inhaling told her he was stunned. He'd always liked Sean. "How badly is he hurt?"

"Not life-threatening. I got the bullet out, but combined with his broken foot, he's in no shape for a manhunt."

"I see. I don't suppose there's a chance you could talk him into going back to the Highlands to heal?"

The Highlands. She felt a sharp stab of pain. "Is that where he's been all this time?"

"Hasn't he told you anything?"

"No." Unable to keep the bitterness from her voice, Natalie sighed, aware of Sean listening. "Sean has said precious little about what he's been doing since he 'died.'"

Silence fell while her father digested this. "I'm sorry," he finally said. "I promise you, if I'd known, I would have moved heaven and hell to get you to him."

"I know." Tiredly, Natalie bit back a sharp retort, concentrating on sounding calm, cool and collected, as an expert field operative should. "I'm surprised Corbett didn't tell you."

Her father's deep chuckle reassured her. "You know how he is. He only reveals what he wants, when he wants. I'm sure he believed this was in your best interest."

"Maybe. But I would have liked a say in deciding that."

"I know. But you've got to move forward, Natalie. Whatever you decide about Sean, you've got to go on with your life."

Easy for him to say. But he was right, as usual.

Blinking back tears and swallowing against the hot ache in her throat, Natalie realized her hand was beginning to go numb from her white-knuckled grip on the phone. She relaxed her fingers and straightened her shoulders.

"I'm trying, Papa," she whispered.

"Good." After exchanging a few more pleasantries, her father rang off. Natalie closed the phone and looked up to find Sean watching her.

"Papa said you've been living in the Highlands."

Expression shuttered, he nodded. "Yes."

She'd only been there once, and he'd taken her. Her first impression had been of chilly damp mystery—the land shrouded itself in mist, hiding its secrets.

"If I remember correctly, you didn't see much of the scenery when we were there," he drawled.

Her cheeks warmed. "True." They'd been newly married and had spent the entire time in bed. From the way Sean's eyes darkened, she knew he remembered, too.

"I never forgot," he said. "As I matter of fact, I bought a cottage in a glen near where we stayed."

Helpless to move, she could only stare. "Why, Sean? Why?"

"It's beautiful there. Peaceful. No bloodshed or gunshots or murder. Just sheep and goats and the occasional bark of a collie."

"You sound as though you made a home there."

"In a way. But my cottage always missed something."

She didn't want to ask—but she had to. "What? What were you missing there?"

"You."

For the space of several heartbeats they stared at each other, his gaze full of longing, making her wonder if the same need showed in her eyes.

Once, they wouldn't have hesitated. Sex had been a balm on anything, a mind-blotting sort of plaster they'd used to fill the cracks in their relationship. And there had been fractures, she realized now. She'd been too blind to see them or, if she'd noticed at all, she'd believed herself too happy to care.

But what about Sean? Had these small fissures become a huge crevice to him? Had this been why he hadn't trusted her enough, why he'd felt he had to do something as drastic as fake his own death?

Second chances were hard to come by, and she refused to begin even the possibility of healing by using sex as a balm. Not this time. Not ever again.

Tossing her cell phone to Sean, she climbed out of bed. "I've got the first shower. If Corbett calls back, talk to him."

Chapter 7

As the door closed behind Natalie, Sean sighed. He felt like an idiot, mooning after her when she continued to make it clear she wanted nothing to do with him.

Yet he'd seen her when she didn't know he was watching, when she let her guard down.

She wanted him as badly as he craved her.

This, and only this, kept his hope alive. Sex between them had always been out of this world.

The shower started and he allowed himself the fantasy of joining her. Once, they'd taken turns surprising the other, slipping in the tub and playing with the soap. He grew hard just thinking about it.

If he kept this up, he'd have to make his shower an icy-cold one.

Natalie's cell phone rang, distracting him. For half a second, he debated ignoring it and letting her return the call, but he snatched it up and said hello.

Corbett's clipped British accent boomed through the earpiece. While Sean spoke with him, he heard Natalie turn off the shower. A mental image of drying her with a fluffy white towel had to be pushed away as Sean tried to concentrate on listening to his former boss.

Corbett rang off and Sean closed the phone as Natalie emerged from the bathroom, finger-brushing her damp hair. She glanced at him, noticed him holding her phone, and froze. "Did he call?"

"Yeah, that was Corbett. He's arranged a drop-off for us."

She visibly relaxed. "I hope he's providing more weapons."

"Yes, and other supplies. He specifically mentioned a laptop."

Her smile made him ache. "Wow, that was fast. Where's he leaving it?"

"Bus station, downtown. In about forty-five minutes."

"That's so clichéd it works." She laughed, then bent over to shake out her short locks. When she straightened, her hair stood out from her head in wanton disarray.

He couldn't stop staring at her. She looked like a beautiful, exotic stranger.

"What?" She lifted a brow. "Why are you looking at me like that?"

"I can't get used to you with red hair."

Her smile faded. He could have sworn she looked wounded for half a second, before she lifted one shoulder in what might have passed for a carefree shrug if he hadn't known her. "I know I look better as a blonde, but my hair color doesn't matter right now."

Ah, but it did. Only he couldn't tell her. He'd learned to paint, alone in his remote crofter's cottage. Amateurish, true, but every canvas had come alive with her face, her eyes, her smile. And her silky hair the bright color of sunshine. He'd painted the true her, letting the images serve as a reminder of the short time in his life when he'd been the happiest.

He'd loved her more than he'd ever loved anything, before and since.

But she knew none of this and never would. He forced his own face into a nonchalant expression. "Give me five minutes in the bathroom and I'll be ready, too."

When she didn't answer, he hobbled to the bathroom door, feeling like a lovesick fool.

The area around the bus station smelled of diesel. They parked two blocks away and Natalie got out. She walked on the opposite side of the street while

Sean parked since he couldn't walk. Pretending only a cursory look at Sean, Natalie gave him a quick nod as he went in, limping in his cast. Natalie waited, counted to ten, then crossed the street with a crowd, her bulky sweater and sturdy boots nondescript, her dark-red hair making her blend in with everyone else. She kept one hand in her pocket, where she'd stuck her pistol. Just in case.

While Sean was inside the bus station, Natalie remained outside, scanning the inevitable group of vagrants and panhandlers hanging around the front. Assassins could easily hide among them, and no one would notice. Well—she wrinkled her nose— except for the smell.

She kept her back to the brick as a safety precaution. Casually, pretending to be taking in the scenery, she watched people hurrying past. In reality she was searching for anything or anyone the slightest bit out of place. She felt horribly exposed. A shooter could appear from any direction, under the cover of the crowd and the noise, and begin firing. Innocent people would be hurt.

She breathed a sigh of relief when, a few minutes later, Sean emerged, carrying a large black duffel bag. He hobbled down the street without even glancing at her.

Again, Natalie counted to ten and then sauntered off as though she wasn't following him or even heading any place in particular. She stopped to peer in shop windows and lifted her chin to breathe in the scent of fresh-made scones from a bakery. Just an everyday citizen, out for a stroll on a chilly autumn day.

No one shot at her. Must be her lucky day.

When she reached the car, Sean already had it running. Slipping into the passenger seat, she secured her seat belt and locked her door as they took off. He drove slowly, not wanting to attract attention.

"Corbett came through. Though I wasn't able to spend much time checking out the contents of the bag, Corbett's pretty thorough. I'm sure we've got what we need. Money, weapons, food."

"Don't forget my computer." Leaning her head back, she closed her eyes.

"*Our* computer."

Opening her eyes and staring at him, she crossed her arms. "What do you mean? Corbett wants me to work on deciphering some code."

"You aren't the only one he's asked to do something." He grimaced. "I may not be an active employee, but Corbett Lazlo is still the best in the business. When he suggests I do something, I tend to listen."

She sighed. "All right, I'll ask since you apparently aren't going to volunteer. What are you going to do with the laptop?"

"Corbett wants me to try to hack into the SIS system."

This destroyed any sense of relaxation she might have harbored. Appalled, she shook her head. "It's impossible."

"So they tell *you*. But it has been done and I'm pretty good. I've had two years of nothing but practice."

"Pretty good?" She snorted. "Hackers have been trying for years. Whatever kind of firewall SIS has in place is top-notch."

With a grin, he shrugged. "I'm not trying to get into the supersecured area, just far enough to wreak a little havoc. All I can do is try."

"True. Say you do succeed. What then?"

"Corbett thinks we should set a trap. It's highly likely the mole's still got people there." Steering around a sharp curve, he shot her a look. "What about you? What's this code Corbett wants you to crack?"

Reaching into her backpack, she withdrew a small plastic case. "Corbett wants me to compare his code to this one."

She opened the case to show him the tiny flash drive. "It's the code I was working on at headquarters, the one I'd brought home with me the night my team was slaughtered. As you probably know, we're forbidden to take anything out of the lab. So no one at SIS knows I have it."

"That's not like you. Or," he amended, "at least not the way I remember you. That's a safety precaution."

"Yes, but not following that particular rule just

might save my life if I can finish decoding this. Someone sent assassins to kill us all. And to destroy the code."

Traffic had slowed, the car was inching along in a line of others. "It was my time off. I decided to take a spontaneous trip to Glasgow. I saw no need to explain my whereabouts. So the assassins didn't know where to find me."

"You've changed."

The blunt assessment should have wounded her. Once, maybe. Not now. "I know. But after you...died, I decided I no longer wanted to color inside the lines." She shot him a grin, her best imitation of his own cocky one. "It worked. My success rate went way up. I've been promoted twice, most recently to team leader. So, if I've changed, I think it's for the better."

He went silent, considering. To her disgust she found herself hoping he'd agree.

Instead, he asked another question. "How do you know they even looked for you?"

"They destroyed my flat. I'd taken the code with me, so I don't think they're aware I have it."

One corner of Sean's mouth quirked up in a half smile. "I'm glad they didn't get you."

"Yeah. That way you didn't have to fake your death for nothing." Bitterness again leaked through her voice. While she wished she could have sounded impersonal, she couldn't help it. This was Sean. He should understand how she felt.

Once, he would have. Back when they'd allowed emotion and hot, wild sex to be the basis for their marriage. She hadn't even known she'd wanted more, until now.

He took her hand, covering it with his. Staring down at their intertwined fingers, she tried to regain her equilibrium. She'd always loved his hands— masculine and callused. The roughness of his skin gave her a sense of protection, or had, once.

Now, his touch only made her hurt and angry.

She pulled her hand away and took a deep breath. "Are you sure Corbett was able to send us a laptop?"

"Yep." He jerked his thumb toward the duffel bag in the backseat. "The laptop's in there—I checked."

"What about an Internet connection?" Keeping focused on business would be the only thing that could keep her from crying.

Sean seemed to understand. "Corbett said it would have wireless. All I have to do is find a hot spot, and I can work."

Of course he'd go first. His job involved a bait-and-wait situation, while hers would be time-consuming and tricky.

Not to mention the fact that deciphering code required intense concentration. She found it far too difficult to concentrate with him around.

Still, she hadn't gotten to be a team leader without understanding how to work well on a team.

"While you're trying to hack into my employer's database, what should I do?"

The grateful look he sent her wasn't lost on her. She was astonished to realize he'd thought she would argue.

"Play lookout, of course. Stop the bad guys before they get to me. Once I get inside the system, I can't be interrupted."

He spoke like it was a done deal. "Pretty confident, aren't you?"

"I told you, I'm pretty good." He lifted one shoulder in a shrug. "Let's just say I've perfected my computer skills over the last two years."

Like an arrow straight to her heart. Another reminder that he'd lived an entire life without her, while she'd dedicated herself to her job and had barely lived at all.

Correction, she thought grimly. She'd learned to live for her work and nothing else.

A honking horn brought her out of her reverie.

"Do you think there's been an accident?"

He checked his watch. "No. Just normal rush-hour traffic. Help me look for a hot spot or a place that advertises an Internet connection."

"There." She pointed. Someone had converted an old church into a trendy coffee shop. Sean swung out of the traffic and into a small lot across the street from the stone building. He found a spot and parked, leaving the engine idling while he leaned over the seat and rummaged in the duffel bag.

"Here we go." He pulled out a smallish laptop. "State-of-the-art. That's good."

Her fingers itched to examine the machine, but she wisely held her tongue. "Good luck. What kind of time are you going to get once you're in?"

"Pretty confident of my abilities, aren't you?"

Throwing her own words right back at her. She couldn't help but smile. "Maybe your self-assurance is contagious. How about an answer? Once you get into the SIS system, what then? What kind of a trap?"

"I'll figure that out once I'm in the system. Until I see what's involved, I have no idea." He got out of the car. "Wait here."

As he'd no doubt known she would, she bristled. "I'd rather go in."

"You'd be a better lookout in the car."

"And you'd be trapped inside, alone. A sitting duck."

"Better one than both of us."

She pushed open her door. "Don't start that."

"Start what?"

"Trying to protect me."

He glared at her as she brushed past him. "I don't like this," he growled, catching up and taking her arm.

Shaking free, she gave him her sweetest, most fake, smile. "Then why don't we both just sit in the car? You'd have more privacy."

"And we'd also be a helluva lot more noticeable." He held open the café's door for her to pass through. "Plus, I happen to have a craving for a strong cup of coffee."

The robust aroma inside tickled her nose. She licked her lips. She'd always loved the scent of fresh coffee. "I could go for a café mocha."

He flashed her the grin that had always made her knees go weak. "I'll buy you one when I've finished."

"I'll buy my own, thank you."

He shot her a look full of amusement. "Then buy me one, too, sweetheart."

She bit her tongue to keep from telling him not to call her sweetheart. No doubt he knew and was doing it deliberately to bait her. She wouldn't give him the satisfaction of rising to the bait.

Stalking to the counter, she ordered two large mochas. Sean claimed a table near the front, taking a seat with his back to the wall, protecting his computer screen from curious eyes as well as enabling him to watch the door. Exactly where she would have sat, had she been the one working on the laptop.

Once the drinks were ready, she carried them to the table and read the newspaper while he worked. She pretended to be intent on the articles, but continually scanned the door and watched out the window for anything out of the ordinary.

"Bingo," he said softly. Barely twenty minutes had passed. "I'm in."

"No way."

With a quick glance at her over the top of the screen, he grinned. "I told you I was good."

Pretending to scan her newspaper, pretending her heart hadn't skipped a beat at the pure masculinity of his grin, she lazily turned a page before peering at him. "Now you set a trap. In code?"

"In code," he confirmed. "Once it's set, all we can do is wait."

"Good." Folding the paper neatly, she placed it on the table and took a long drink of her coffee. "I can't wait to get started on *my* work."

"Not here."

"Of course not." But his words made her want to snatch the computer away from him and start working immediately.

Natalie sighed. She had to do something about this crazy urge to do the exact opposite of everything Sean said. Not only was it childish, it wasn't safe for either of them.

She drew a deep breath. She also needed to do something about this sexual tension. Constant arousal and unrequited need didn't do much for a girl's mood.

If only she could stop wanting him.

She almost laughed. Almost. She knew all she had to do was initiate lovemaking and Sean would do the rest. Such a solution might help one problem, but would only exacerbate another.

Making love would only pretend to strengthen ties that had become nearly nonexistent. And her feelings for her husband were about much more than lust and desire.

If only she could stop loving him.

Grabbing her half-finished coffee, she followed him out the door.

They found a quiet inn a few miles from downtown, in a nontourist part of town.

Sean called Corbett while Natalie was in the bathroom. Quickly, he brought the older man up to speed. "I'll check the system frequently to see if he takes my bait."

"Excellent." Corbett sounded stressed—unusual for him. "How is everything else going with you two?"

Though he knew the other man meant relationship-wise, Sean pretended not to understand. "Never a dull moment, that's for sure. This is getting ridiculous, since we can't even seem to get a handle on who the Hungarian is using to take us out. I almost feel like he put up reward money and every Tom, Dick and Harry is taking potshots at us."

"What do you mean?"

"Let's see." Sean ticked the items off on his fingers. "We've been shot at, had grenades lobbed at us, buildings blown up, associates murdered and we have no more information than we did when we started."

"Information about…"

"About anything." Sean clenched his teeth, holding back though he wanted to explode. "If this was a regular mission, with a team and a well-thought-out plan, that would be one thing. But there's just the two of us, wandering around with blindfolds on. Sure, me hacking into the SIS system was a good plan, and Natalie is trying to decipher that code, but we need to get our act together before someone gets killed."

"I understand."

"No, Corbett. I don't think you do." Sean's temper flared. "Natalie has been through enough."

"As have you." The other man's voice was serious and quiet. "Get a grip. I want the man responsible just as much as you do."

Corbett sighed. "Someone is trying to undermine the Lazlo Group, Sean. I've got all kinds of operations going wrong and operatives going dead. Between the mole in the SIS and the mole at Lazlo everything is being disrupted. Maybe it's the work of the Hungarian, maybe it's not. But we won't know that until we find him, and stop him."

"Why?" Sean had been wanting to ask this question ever since he'd first come to work for the Lazlo Group. "What did you do to the Hungarian to make him hate you so much?"

"Natalie asked me the same thing."

"Did you answer her?"

"No."

"Are you going to answer me?"

"I doubt it. That's a long story and things are too crazy here to go into it now. Remember, I've lost people too." A hint of anger colored Corbett's cultured voice.

Sean apologized. "I'm sorry. There's a lot of tension between Natalie and me. This is hell for both of us. I don't know why you thought we could work together."

"She needed help and asked for the best. You're the best."

"Once, maybe. Not now."

Corbett ignored him. "Plus I've gotten tired of you pining away for her up there in that godforsaken cottage you call home."

Sean knew better than to argue. What Corbett said was the indisputable truth. "True, I missed her. But I didn't realize she'd hate me when she saw me again."

"Does she, Sean? There's a fine line between love and hate."

"Spare me the platitudes. I've seen how she is when she loves. Trust me, this is hate."

"She's hurting."

Like they both weren't? "Defending her?"

With a sigh, Corbett conceded the point. "You know Nat's like a daughter to me." Which was why Corbett had asked Sean to help protect her to begin with.

OFFICIAL OPINION POLL

ANSWER 3 QUESTIONS AND WE'LL SEND YOU
4 FREE BOOKS AND A FREE GIFT!

0074823 |||||||||||| |||||||| |||||||

FREE GIFT CLAIM # 3953

YOUR OPINION COUNTS!

Please tick TRUE or FALSE below to express your opinion about the following statements:

Q1 Do you believe in "true love"?

"TRUE LOVE HAPPENS ONLY ONCE IN A LIFETIME."

○ TRUE
○ FALSE

Q2 Do you think marriage has any value in today's world?

"YOU CAN BE TOTALLY COMMITTED TO SOMEONE WITHOUT BEING MARRIED."

○ TRUE
○ FALSE

Q3 What kind of books do you enjoy?

"A GREAT NOVEL MUST HAVE A HAPPY ENDING."

○ TRUE
○ FALSE

YES, I have scratched the area below.

Please send me the 4 **FREE BOOKS** and **FREE GIFT** for which I qualify. I understand I am under no obligation to purchase any books, as explained on the back of this card.

I8KI

Mrs/Miss/Ms/Mr _____ Initials _____

BLOCK CAPITALS PLEASE

Surname _____

Address _____

_____

Postcode _____

The Reader Service™ — Here's how it works:

NO STAMP NEEDED!

THE READER SERVICE™
FREE BOOK OFFER
FREEPOST CN81
CROYDON
CR9 3WZ

NO STAMP
NECESSARY
IF POSTED IN
THE U.K. OR N.I.

About to respond, Sean winced when the smoke alarm went off. The high-pitched wailing made hearing anything else impossible.

"I've got to go." Sean disconnected the call. He didn't smell smoke, but that didn't mean a hell of a lot. With the constant attacks on them—and their enemies' disconcerting way of tracking them down—he wouldn't be surprised to learn the building was on fire.

The bathroom door opened. With no makeup on, Natalie looked impossibly young.

"What's going on?" she yelled. "Where's the fire?"

He could tell she'd changed hastily since her top was inside out. He grabbed the laptop then her arm and led the way to the door. "I don't know, but we'd better get out."

She balked. "What if it's a trap?"

"What if it's not?"

Outside, the air was bracingly chilly. The wind coming out of the north felt like ice. They kept close to the building, looking for smoke.

Other people poured from the building and stood around in clusters, some looking confused, others angry or bemused. All of them looked cold.

Fire engines pulled up in front of the inn.

"There's no smoke," someone said.

"I don't see anything." Sean squinted into the early-afternoon glare. The bright sunlight seemed at odds with the bitter cold. "No smoke. No fire."

"False alarm." One of the bellmen came outside and shouted. "Once the fire department gives the okay, everyone can return to their rooms. It should be just a few minutes."

"Good." Wrapping her arms around herself, Natalie shivered. "Damn. I wish I'd grabbed my coat."

He pulled her into his arms. "Come here." When she hesitated, he shook his head. "No funny business, Nat. Shared body heat is better. You'll be warmer this way."

She relaxed against him, but only slightly. "Have you checked out the parking lot?"

"We're on the north side of the building. All the cars are parked on the south. Whoever pulled the fire alarm wanted us out of the building, but why?"

"The code!" The bellman indicated they could return to their rooms and she ran for the entrance. "Maybe they think I left it in the room."

He limped after her, struggling to keep up. "Did you?"

"Of course not," she scoffed. "It's with me. I never let it out of my sight. And Corbett's info is on the laptop."

"How would they know you have either of them?"

"That's what I'd like to know." Shooting him an exasperated look, she yanked open the side door and quickly entered the registration area.

"Nat, wait for me. We're a team, remember? For now, you're supposed to work with me, to trust me." The instant he spoke he knew he'd made a major mistake.

"Been there, done that. No thanks." She stopped a moment and looked at him, her face unreadable, her mouth set in a grim line that was totally unlike the Natalie he knew and loved.

"Nat, wait…"

Ignoring him, she kept going.

Since he had no choice, he followed, grabbing her arm. "You can't just walk away from me if we're going to work together…"

"Work?" She spun to face him and he was startled to see tears in her caramel eyes. "This has nothing to do with work."

Sean took a deep breath. "Look, Nat, I know you'll never forgive me for what I did two years ago. I can explain my reasons until I'm blue in the face, and you won't understand."

"I swear if you say it's time to put the past behind us and move forward, I'm going to puke all over you."

Since that was exactly what he'd been planning to say, he said nothing. Instead, he kept his mouth shut and stared at her.

She stared back, the coldness of her expression at war with the pain in her eyes.

"You've gone on with your life, have you?" he finally asked.

"As best I could."

"You've found someone else then?"

For the space of one heartbeat, two, she said nothing. Finally, she made an odd little sound and shook her head. "You don't know how badly I'd like to lie and tell you yes, I've found someone else."

"Like Dennie Pachla, the doctor?" he suggested, hating himself for asking but wanting, needing to know.

"He's a friend." Her voice was tired. "Like Auggie. I don't know why I'm telling you this, but there's been no one else."

Some devil urged him on. "Why not?" he pushed. "Two years is plenty of time for a grief-stricken widow to move on with her life."

She looked down, twisting her hands together. When she finally raised her head, the anguished look on her face made him feel as if he'd twisted the knife.

"Do you know what it's like to love someone so much that every beat of your heart echoes theirs?" Her voice broke, but she didn't cry.

Before he could answer, she continued.

"Do you have any idea, any idea at all, what it's like to *love someone that much* and then have them ripped out of your arms?"

"Yes," he said quietly. "I do."

"I don't think so." She held up her hand when he would have argued. "Because honestly, Sean, if you had, you would have known I nearly followed you to the grave."

Shocked, stunned, he shook his head. "You mean you...? Corbett never told me."

"Corbett doesn't know. Would it have made a difference, Sean? Would you have shown up at my funeral?"

"How can you ask such a thing?" Now, when he'd thought he had nothing left unbroken, the last bit of his heart shattered. "I can't believe you tried to—"

She shrugged. "It wasn't intentional, Sean. I was hurting and my doctor had prescribed pills. I suppose I knew I shouldn't mix antidepressants and alcohol, but I only intended to have one drink." She took a deep breath. "Next thing I knew, I woke up in a hospital."

This he couldn't wrap his mind around. "I had no idea."

"How could you? You were dead."

The repercussions of his lie had been worse and had spread wider than he'd ever imagined. "I couldn't have lived with myself if you'd died," he said.

"How do you think I felt?" The sheer anguish in her voice struck him raw. And as she turned away, he wanted only to wrap her tight in his arms and tell her he'd never let her go again.

Chapter 8

Moving with the others down the long hallway, Natalie knew when she saw the partially opened door of their room that they had been right.

Whoever had pulled the alarm had been in their room. Had trashed it.

"The only other person I've told about the code is Corbett. This must be the work of the Lazlo Group mole."

"That's possible." Standing in the doorway, Sean nodded. "What about your friend Auggie?"

"Auggie's a good guy. He wouldn't do this."

Sean shook his head, as though he didn't completely agree. "What a frigging mess."

The room looked like a jacked-up demon on meth had torn through it. Natalie couldn't even begin to envision explaining this to the inn management. Hopefully, they would just assume it was a break-in and since their room was near the exit, it had been the easiest to target.

"I know." Pacing from one end of the room to the other, Natalie looked for any sign to indicate who the culprit was. "They must have been pretty pissed off when they didn't find it."

"Obviously."

She fingered the tiny flash drive. "Of course they didn't realize this baby stays with me everywhere I go."

The next morning, Natalie tried to avoid looking at Sean, as though he could read in her eyes the dreams that had tormented her in the darkest part of the night. Pleasant dreams, indeed.

She'd known she wanted him, of course. But she wasn't in the habit of lying to herself, and what she hadn't realized was exactly *how much* she wanted him. Like a craving, an addiction, her desire for him never left her.

Worse, she knew *why*. Making love was exactly that to her—two people, madly in love, celebrating with their bodies. Sean had been her one and only and she'd come to him untouched, a virgin.

She was still untouched, by choice. If she

couldn't love someone else as much as she'd loved Sean, she didn't think she would ever know another's body either.

Sex to her was not a recreational pastime, a fleeting pleasure. Sex to her was akin to the deepest baring of the soul.

In the harsh light of the morning, she had to look herself in the mirror and ask herself a question. Did she want to go the rest of her life knowing Sean was alive, out there in the world without her, and imagine him wrapped in another woman's arms?

She'd been given a second chance, another opportunity to be with the only man she had ever loved.

But could she ever forget and forgive him for what he'd done?

She didn't think she could.

Waking up and seeing Natalie in the morning was another form of torture for Sean. He couldn't tear his gaze away from her. With her short, tousled hair and heavy-lidded eyes, she looked as though her dreams had been similar to his.

Sex and more sex.

Shaking his head, he flipped open his cell phone.

"Who are you calling?" her sleep-groggy voice asked.

"Corbett. I want to get some answers. We need to find out where that leak is. Find out if someone knows about your bootlegged code and how they're keeping tabs on us."

Four rings, five, then the call went to voice mail. Sean hung up without leaving a message.

Natalie grimaced, got out of bed and took out her own cell phone. "I'm going to make a few calls of my own. I'm just as tired of this as you are."

But she had no better luck. Sean listened as she left two separate messages. "Who'd you call?"

"Auggie and Dennie. Auggie's one of the best undercover ops SIS has."

He'd suspected as much. But the handsome doctor? "What about Dennie?" He tried to keep the jealousy from his voice.

"He does occasional work for us. For the Lazlo Group, too." She shot him a wry look. "You'd know that if you hadn't been gone so long."

Sean bit back a retort. "How close are the two of you?"

Shaking her head, Natalie walked to the window. "You don't have a right to ask that question."

"Maybe not, but I'm asking anyway."

She sighed. "Drop it, okay?"

Her nonanswer told him she had something to hide.

"Have you and the doctor…?" Swallowing, he tried to find the right words without being crude.

"Sean, I said drop it." Her cutting tone told him

she was furious. "My private life is none of your business. You died, remember?"

He swallowed his own anger, not wanting the conversation to degenerate into an out-and-out fight.

His hopes and dreams—all but vanished—came back to him in startling clarity. He'd had a future, once. He'd envisioned bright-haired children, laughing and playing. A white picket fence. The way Natalie's eyes glowed amber when she was happy. Laughter instead of tears. Joy instead of grief. Love instead of pain.

So much had been lost, taken from him because of a youthful error in judgment.

How did one right such a wrong? Could he even go back, make another grab for that elusive brass ring?

Did they even have a chance?

"Fine. My apologies." He dipped his chin. "We'll keep it strictly business. Tell me what you think Auggie and Dennie can find out that we or Corbett can't?"

"You never know." A tinge of relief colored her voice, which only irritated him further as she continued. "Auggie's good—he keeps his ear to the ground. And Dennie—he's everywhere. He's one of the few doctors still willing to do house calls."

"Is he part of your intelligence network?"

"No, though he's a trusted contact. And," she shot him a meaningful look, "a good friend. I've even heard it rumored he's getting set up to do some doctoring among the Hungarian's people."

Despite himself, Sean was impressed. "That would be quite a coup for your intelligence network."

"Yeah, it would." Her smile looked tentative, but at least it was a smile. "Auggie and I are both very proud of him."

Auggie and Nat. Geez, he had it bad. Just thinking about the two of them together rankled. Oblivious, Natalie continued. "Once Auggie calls back, we might have a bit more information to go on. I'm getting tired of running around in circles."

She had a point. "True," he conceded as he got out of bed and gathered his clothes. "Let's see what they are able to find out. But for now, I'm going to grab a shower. Then we should get some breakfast and you can keep working on those codes."

"Sounds like a plan," she said and smiled at him a bit sadly, as she lightly touched the antique armoire and ran her fingers along the curved wooden back of a Queen Anne replica chair.

He instantly thought of the home they'd once shared, and how she'd loved to antique-shop, filling their rooms with cherished finds. He'd come to appreciate the eclectic mix as well, loving the variety, seeing it as an extension of her complex personality.

How much he'd loved her. How much they'd loved each other. Did she really believe such a love could ever die?

Before he said or did something he'd later regret, he headed for the attached bathroom and a nice, long shower.

Turning the water up as hot as he could stand, Sean took his time, standing under the pulsing stream. Each swipe of the soapy washcloth reminded him of Natalie's hands, soft and silky on his rough skin. By the time he'd finished cleaning, his arousal was nearly unbearable in its intensity.

He had two choices—turn the faucet to cold or take matters into his own hands.

Stubborn and hurting, he refused to do either. Instead, he forced his mind onto other matters and finished his shower. By the time he turned off the water, he'd nearly returned to normal.

Until he opened the shower curtain, reached for his towel and saw her.

She'd undressed in the steamy bathroom, and her pale skin glistened with the damp heat. Unclothed, she let him look at her, no false modesty between them, her breasts high and firm over her narrow waist and the curve of her hips, her chin lifted proudly. No guilt or remorse darkened her expression.

She'd come for him. Why now? Yet she had, and whatever her reasons, he would take her any way he could get her. He'd worry about the *why* later.

"Natalie?" Her name rolled off his tongue like a prayer. She nearly overwhelmed him, there so close, naked, looking better than she had the thousand times he'd dreamed of her. Her scent, musky and full of desire, made him feel as if he was drowning. The look in her eyes, hot and sensual, reflected his own emotions—so much more than simple need or lust or desire—and he couldn't be sure he wasn't imagining this.

Natalie wanted him. Finally he could join his body to hers once again.

For two long years he'd thought of little else. Natalie, his Natalie. The woman he'd been willing to die for.

His breath caught in his throat. Somehow, he choked out her name again.

She held out her arms. Without hesitation, he went to her, crushing her to his chest so she could feel the rapid thud of his heartbeat, moving them both out of the bathroom, toward the bed. His body primed, he tried to hold away from her, not wanting to frighten her with the strength of his arousal.

He should have known better. This Natalie, the adventurous Super-spy, wasn't afraid of anything.

Both hands on his backside, she pulled him to her. Together, they tumbled backward onto the bed.

Their mouths touched. Locked. Greedy, he tried to rein in his passion, but two years of dreaming and longing and missing her had taken their toll.

He didn't think he'd ever been so aroused. So ready. Fleetingly, he wondered how he'd lived without her. Then she took him in her hands and he lost all capacity for rational thought.

Just as he pushed her away, unable to bear any more without exploding, her cell phone rang.

"Ignore it," she murmured, shimmying into position over him, poised to take him deep inside her. "They'll call back."

"Good advice," he muttered. One thrust and he'd be in, yet for some reason, he hesitated.

As soon as her cell quit ringing, his began.

Reluctantly, he glanced at it. "It must be important," he growled. Body throbbing, he cursed once more before snatching the phone and flipping it open. "Hello?"

"Sean, I have some bad news," Corbett's voice came over the line. "Phillip's missing."

"Missing?"

"Who?" Natalie mouthed, suddenly alert.

"Your father."

All the blood drained from her face.

Gripping the phone, Sean swallowed. "What do you mean, missing? He's in a wheelchair and when he goes out he's driven by one of your men. You should know where he is at all times."

"His van and my man are missing also." Corbett sounded weary and furious, all at the same time.

"What?" None of this made sense. "Why?"

"I don't know. I've got people working on finding that out."

Sean raised his head to find Natalie watching him, an expression of concern on her lovely face. His gut clenched as he remembered his own family and how he'd tried to shield her from the terrible truth.

He could not shield her from this.

"Let me talk to Natalie," Corbett said.

"Not now." Sean took a deep breath. "We'll call you back." Without giving Corbett a chance to disagree, he disconnected the call.

"What happened to my father?"

He told her all he knew, holding her tightly.

In shock, she let him. When she raised her head, the blank look she gave him clawed at his heart. "Is there something else you haven't told me?"

"No."

Her frown made it plain she didn't believe him. "No ransom note?"

"Corbett's looking into it. You know how close the two of them are."

With a sound of pain, she twisted out of his arms, got off the bed and grabbed her clothes.

"I want to talk to Corbett." Opening her own phone, she punched in the number.

Corbett must have been waiting by the phone for her call. Sean watched while Natalie listened, the anguished expression on her face making him ache.

"Wait a minute, Corbett," she said, clutching the phone so tightly her knuckles showed white. "Let me put you on speaker so Sean can hear, too." She pressed a button. "All right. Go ahead."

"I've got two people working full-time on finding him."

"Who?" Sean asked.

"Martin Routh and Catherine Cordasic."

Sean started. "One of *the* Cordasics?" Widely known in the international espionage community, the Cordasics were a highly respected family of spies whose lineage dated back to the eighteenth century.

"Yes. She's working as an independent contractor, at my request."

Sean whistled. "You must have pulled a few strings."

Natalie cleared her throat. "Famous spies mean nothing to me unless they find my father. Tell me the truth, Corbett. You and my father didn't have a clandestine conversation about the need for him to go into hiding, did you?"

"Of course not." Corbett's icy voice turned positively glacial. "I'm afraid your father's disappearance might be tied up with the Hungarian."

Sean choked back a curse. Not again. He didn't know how he'd live through more senseless slaughter.

Natalie strode over to the window, gazing out. "What would the Hungarian want with him? Dad's been retired for years now. He's not involved in any of this."

"No, but you are," Corbett answered.

Natalie looked at Sean. The look on her face was so bleak, he knew the words Corbett didn't speak tasted like ashes in her mouth.

She swallowed. "You think they took him to get to me. To use him as bait."

"Unfortunately, yes."

"My father's the only family I have left in this world, Corbett. You know that."

"Of course I do." The older man's tone was equally firm. "He's my good friend as well."

"Do you think it's possible Phillip simply decided to begin his own investigation?" Sean asked.

No one discounted the idea. Despite his handicap, Natalie's father was an extremely determined man.

"Either way, I think they have him. He was mentioned in the e-mail message I intercepted this morning."

"From who?" Sean asked.

"One of my old adversaries in contact with the Hungarian."

Sean froze. "What did it say?"

Corbett cleared his throat. "Something about upping the stakes. The last sentence said, 'One down, three more to go.'"

"Three?" Natalie piped up. "There are only two—myself and Sean."

"And me," Corbett said quietly. "I make three."

"Damn it. There's something we're missing. Some piece to a cryptic jigsaw puzzle."

"The code," Natalie breathed. "I've got to decipher this code."

Sean knew Natalie had always loved jigsaw puzzles. Growing up, her father had made sure she had a steady supply of them. Sean had continued the tradition. He'd always said her aptitude with puzzles was one of the reasons she was so good at cracking codes.

"It's time to tell us everything, Corbett." Natalie's quiet voice was edged with steel. "Obviously, something happened in the past to make this guy hate you."

Corbett sighed. Sean could picture him running his hand through his perfectly cut hair. "My operations have angered hundreds, maybe thousands of people over the years. Such is the high price of freedom."

"If he so much as harms a hair on my father's head…"

"Stay calm, Natalie. For now, we can't assume the worst."

"How can I not?" Natalie said, her even tone somehow more horrible than a scream. "My father's missing. Until he's found, I have no choice but to assume the worst."

Closing the phone, she placed it back on the dresser. When her gaze met Sean's he saw her eyes had gone blank and guarded. "I don't believe this."

"Unfortunately, I do. The Hungarian will stop at nothing to get what he wants."

Expression thoughtful, Natalie prowled around the room like an agitated lioness. "Someone, somewhere has to know the Hungarian's identity. Someone has to have seen his face."

Sean's heart stopped. He cleared his throat, forcing himself to sound nonchalant. "I *have* seen his face, and I actually know his first name. But I've never been able to learn his surname."

"You?" She stared. "You've never mentioned this before. When did you see him? Does Corbett know?"

He struggled to sound indifferent. "I've never told him."

"Why not?"

Taking a deep breath, he watched her cross her arms. Carefully—he knew he had to tread carefully.

"Because there's a part of my past I didn't want him to know."

"Or me?" She straightened her shoulders.

"Or you," he agreed, feeling as if he'd hammered another nail in his own coffin. "I'm sorry, Nat. But there's something else I have to tell you."

Chapter 9

"I've had enough of your secrets." She hadn't meant to raise her voice, yet here she was, shouting like a fishwife. Still, yelling felt damn good. Maybe it was about time she screamed at him. He'd certainly earned it.

Despite this, she took a deep breath and deliberately lowered her voice. "You keep pulling them out of your hat like rabbits, one right after the other, until I wonder if you even know where they begin and end."

God, she hadn't thought it would still hurt, hadn't even thought that she could hurt this much. Yet, watching the wary expression on his face, she wondered if she'd ever even known the real Sean.

"I told you some of the truth yesterday. And you didn't want to hear the rest so I held back to protect you."

"I'm not a child, Sean." Her voice rose again. "I'm your wife. Or *was* your wife. There weren't supposed to be secrets between us. I can only take so much."

She shook her head, the anger leaching out of her as rapidly as it had come, replaced by a deep, deep sadness. "Is there anything you've ever told me that wasn't false?"

This time when he looked at her, she saw her own sorrow reflected in his eyes. "As I matter of fact, there is. When I said I love you and that everything I did was for you, I told the truth."

Though she wanted to run and put some distance between them, she didn't move, but knew he'd seen the disbelief in her face. "And now?"

"Are you sure you can handle this?"

Clenching her teeth, she nodded. "What could be worse than learning your own husband pretended to be dead for two years?"

Hurt flashed across his face, but he let her barb go.

"I tried to tell you this before," he reminded her. "But you said you'd had enough truth for one day."

"I'm ready now. I wasn't then."

"There is another reason the Hungarian wants me dead," Sean said slowly. "You know the story of how Corbett found me?"

"I swear if you tell me that was a lie, I'll—"

"It was partial truth. I had just graduated from university, and I fell in with a bad crowd. I spent a lot of time partying and living in the streets. When I did work, I worked as a dishwasher or a busboy. Corbett used to come into this restaurant all the time. He'd talk to me, ask me questions and listen to me. He made me see I could do better. Finally, he offered me a job."

She inhaled. "Yes, I know. That's the same thing you and Corbett always told me. What part's untrue?"

"Corbett did find me, but someone else found me first."

Not comprehending, Natalie waited. "Who?"

"The Hungarian."

Despite herself, she took a step back. This was Sean. Sean. Who apparently had always been a master at hiding the truth. Could he have sunk any lower?

"You're a double agent? You're the mole inside the Lazlo Group. Oh my God." She couldn't catch her breath. "You not only lied to me, but you lied to Corbett, too? You've double-crossed everyone."

After a moment of stunned silence, Sean laughed. This shocked her even further, though it was a hollow sound. "Come on, Nat. Be realistic. You know better."

"Do I?" She resisted the urge to rub her stinging eyes. "Apparently I don't know you at all."

The guarded expression of mirth that he'd affected vanished. Hurt darkened his eyes. "I know

I hurt you, but I did what I thought was best. For you. So you could live. Now, I might have done things differently, but—"

"The road to hell is paved with good intentions," she cut him off. "Answer the question, Sean. Are you the mole?"

"Of course not. I can't believe you would think such a thing."

"Can't you?" Again her anger, always close to the surface, bubbled up. "Nothing you've told me is true. Why should this be any different?"

He sighed. "I worked for the Hungarian briefly, a long time ago, before I knew any better."

She felt as though she'd been zapped by a Taser. "You...worked for him? Then you know who he is."

"Not really. I told you—I've seen his face. But his real name—no one knows that. We all called him Big V. That was before he became known as the Hungarian."

She had to ask. "What did you do for him? What kind of work?" Praying he wouldn't tell her he'd been the assassin for an organization that bordered on terrorism.

"I did very little work." Brows lowered, he looked annoyed. "Like I keep trying to tell you, I didn't work for him that long. He's the one who arranged the meeting with Corbett. He was aware Corbett liked that restaurant, so he got me a job there and made sure I got Corbett's section. I guess he must have known Corbett would be a sucker for someone like me—a young man with a good education but no direction."

She gaped at him. "You're telling me the Hungarian—"

"Sent me in to take down Corbett. Yes. But I couldn't. Once I got to know him and saw what he was like…"

His voice broke. "So I pretended to be waiting for the right opportunity, which of course never came. Eventually, Big V began to question me, and I broke off all contact."

Now the vendetta made more sense.

"You double-crossed the Hungarian? One of the most powerful underworld bosses in the world?"

He lifted one shoulder in a shrug. "I barely knew him. I worked for him while I was at university. After I graduated, Corbett took me in, taught me the ropes. Helped me believe in myself. I couldn't do what I'd been sent to do."

"Why'd he want to kill Corbett?"

"No clue." Shaking his head, his expression was grim. "But he's hated him for years. Corbett can tell you the exact number of attempts that have been made to kill him over the years."

"And the e-mails? Are they from him, too?"

"I don't think so. I've tried to trace them, but the trail leads right back to the Lazlo Group's server."

She took a deep breath. "All right, so you never

told me. I'll try to deal with that. But why didn't you tell Corbett the truth? He was your mentor."

"Tell him? How could I?" Expression anguished, he took a step toward her, then stopped. "I was afraid. Afraid he'd stop trusting me. Afraid he'd send me back into the streets where I'd be at the complete mercy of the man I betrayed." He sighed. "Then I met you and fell in love. I couldn't go back. I didn't want to go back."

"Didn't you realize if the Hungarian could hate Corbett for years, he could surely want to make you pay, no matter how long it took?"

"At first I didn't. I was young and green. I didn't fully understand how much power Big V had at his disposal. He gave me no warning, nothing. He simply sent his people in and obliterated my entire family. I knew you were next."

"So you 'died.'" Even remembering hurt.

"I had to." The earnestness in his voice made her throat ache. "Don't you understand? You were next. He means to torture and kill everyone I ever cared about."

As if he was the only one who'd suffered.

"I lost the baby." She hadn't meant to say that. Once the words were out, she desperately wanted to call them back. Oddly enough, she felt as though she'd been the one hiding secrets from him.

He froze. "What baby?"

Swallowing, she braced herself to say the words.

Bringing it up again only served to awaken old grief, old pain.

"I was pregnant, Sean. With our child."

"You didn't tell me?"

"I was going to tell you that night, the night you 'died.'" Her voice broke, but she forced herself to continue. "I had everything planned. I thought we could announce it to your entire family together."

The anguish in his face mirrored that in her heart.

"Sweet Jesus…I didn't know."

"It doesn't matter now," she lied. She'd convinced herself she was all right for so long, she didn't dare fall apart now.

Now he did come to her, pulling her into his arms. "Did you tell anyone?"

"Only my father, and I swore him to secrecy." She held herself stiffly, unwilling to take comfort from Sean now, when it was far too late.

"I didn't know," he murmured again, his voice breaking. "God, Nat. I'm terribly, terribly sorry."

"Yeah. Me, too." Pushing him away before she lost control and started weeping, Natalie tried for stoic and settled on disgust. "I've already grieved for him, Sean. Two years ago."

He winced. "Our son?" His voice was hoarse. "You're telling me we would have had a son?"

Managing a nod, she said nothing. She didn't trust herself to speak. Not yet.

He reached for her again. "What you've been through…"

Evading him, she took a step back and shook her head. "I survived. Just like you." Taking a deep breath, irrationally proud that her voice sounded steady, she met his gaze. "About the Hungarian, Sean. Big V. You need to tell Corbett."

"I know." He began to pace, his agitated movements clearly showing his tension. Finally, he ended up facing her, though the length of the room separated them. "I can't tell Corbett. Not now."

"But—"

His expression totally shut down, making him appear cold and remote. A stranger.

"Nat, I've lost everything and everyone I've ever cared about. My entire family, my friends, you. Can't you see that Corbett's all I have left? I don't want to lose him, too."

"He loves you like a son, Sean. You won't lose him."

"No, that's where you're wrong. If he were to find out that I once conspired against him, he'd never forgive—or forget. I know him better than you do."

"I've known Corbett since I was a little girl," she protested. "He and my father grew up together. You know that."

"Maybe he considers you family. But me…" He crossed his arms and shook his head. "He has a strong sense of honor. You've never seen him when he feels someone has betrayed him. I have."

"Do you really think he'd view this as a betrayal? You did nothing."

"No, but I intended to. With him, intent is all that matters." Hands clenched into fists, he took a step toward her and stopped. The agony in his eyes tore at her heart. "Give me your word, Natalie. Give me your word you won't tell him."

She nearly choked. He knew when she promised something, she meant it. It took every ounce of self-restraint she possessed not to point out he wasn't in a position to ask favors of her. Instead, she told him the truth, as she always had in the past. "I don't plan on telling him. That's something you've got to deal with on your own. I won't make it easy for you."

Relief flashed across his handsome face. "Good. Thank you."

"Don't thank me, Sean." She dug out her phone, turning it over in her hand. "You're the one who has to live with yourself, not me."

Again a shadow filled his eyes and she knew he was remembering. Holding her breath, waiting for something—something intangible, something she couldn't put a name to if she tried, she ached. Looking at him, she couldn't help but remember, too.

How much she'd loved this man. How much he'd loved her—or so she'd once believed. His eyes were dark with pain. Tired eyes. Beloved eyes. Still.

Ruthlessly, she pushed the thought away and opened her cell phone.

"Now who are you calling?"

"Auggie again." She frowned. "He never called back. I'm a bit worried. I wonder if he's heard about my father."

This time Auggie answered on the fourth ring. "Nat! How good to hear from you. I'm sorry I never returned your call. Things have been a bit crazy. The bad guys are planning something big and I've been trying to get information on it."

"I know what it is." She took a deep breath. "Aug, they've got my father."

He didn't understand. "What? Who's got your father?"

"We think it's the Hungarian."

"The Hungarian?" Auggie's surprise came clear over the phone. "That doesn't make sense. Why on earth would the Hungarian want your father?"

"We think he wants to use Dad as bait."

"Bait for what?" Auggie sounded grim. As though he meant to wade into the mess, find the Hungarian, and pull him out by the scruff of his fat neck.

Natalie sighed. "That stupid code. The one I copied. And Sean. They want Sean."

"Why? Sean's no threat to them, is he? And you never deciphered their code, so it's worthless." He paused. "Or did you?"

"No, I haven't. Not yet."

"Then why would they want it? Especially if it's their own code?"

"Maybe it's not their code."

"What?" Auggie asked.

She looked at Sean, remembering their conversation. "If these two pieces of code do belong to someone else, maybe the Hungarian wants to decipher them before we do."

"Let me see if I can find out anything. I'll call you back." Auggie hung up.

Sean looked at her, considering. "Where did you get your code?"

"One of our agents brought it in. I don't know where she got it."

"Can you ask her? This could be important."

"She's dead. She got assigned to work on my team, which, as you know, was a death sentence."

Lightly he touched her shoulder. "Don't be so hard on yourself. Try and think. Maybe she might have talked about something minor, something that could give us a hint how she came by that coded message."

Natalie tried to remember if Sonia had mentioned where the code had come from. "Nothing comes to mind."

"Maybe it'll come to you." When he took his hand from her skin, she felt bereft. "In the meantime, I need to call Corbett and see if he can tell me how he came by his coded message."

While Sean talked to Corbett, Natalie wandered the small room, trying to think. So far she hadn't been successful in deciphering an entire word or phrase—she'd been too busy trying to establish an alphabet.

Maybe she'd been going about it the wrong way. Perhaps she needed to treat the coded message as if it were a treasure map.

Wearing circles in the carpet, she paced while she pondered.

"Nat?" Gradually, she became aware of Sean calling her name. She blinked and turned to face him, keeping her expression neutral.

"Corbett's going to research how his man intercepted the code. Unfortunately, that particular agent is also dead, but should have left detailed records. He'll get back to us as soon as he knows."

"Good. In the meantime, I've got to break the code." She grabbed the laptop, opening it and powering it up.

Dimly conscious of Sean gathering his things and leaving to get some breakfast, she brought up the code file. Soon, she was lost in the lines of text, trying to decipher a pattern.

Sean brought her food—coffee and muffins in the morning then later fish and chips. Waving her thanks, she ate absentmindedly, tasting little, unable to shake the feeling that she was on the edge of a major breakthrough.

She worked on the laptop while Sean slept, the tall lamp over the uncomfortable hotel chair her only light. Though urgency drove her, breaking code had always excited her. She suspected this was the reason she was considered one of the best in the world. True, the Lazlo Group had several who were experts, but she'd been at the top of the SIS heap.

Eventually, the letters swam and she blinked. Time to give her eyes a rest. Ten minutes—no more. Then she'd be back at it, even if she had to work straight through the night.

She had to break this code. Their lives—and her father's life—could very well depend on it. Close— she was getting close. She could taste it.

After sunset, she was still hunched over the computer when Sean's cell phone rang. He sat bolt upright, reaching for the phone at the same time as she did. Their hands collided and she drew back first, letting him grab his own phone.

"It's Corbett." Instead of answering privately, he punched the speaker button.

"I've learned where the code came from."

"Where?"

"You remember Kitya, the Hungarian's mistress? Before she died, she stole the Opar diamond from him."

Natalie gasped. "The Opar diamond is just a legend."

"No, it's not." Pacing now, Sean circled the room.

"I'd heard the Hungarian had it, but I wasn't aware the gem had been stolen."

"The Hungarian kept that under wraps. He's been searching for two years. Especially since the stone hasn't been recovered. The coded messages are from Kitya to her lover." Corbett cleared his throat. "A man the Hungarian executed shortly after Kitya's death. The Hungarian believes the messages detail where she hid the diamond."

"And he wants it back."

"Of course," Corbett said in a dry tone. "He'll stop at nothing to get it."

"He can have the damn thing for all I care."

"Natalie." Corbett's voice was harsh, fury barely contained. "You can't let them win. The code is a bargaining chip. Decipher the message and the value is tripled."

"My father—" she swallowed "—could already be dead. You know how this works. What guarantee do we have that he's still alive?"

"Phillip—your father—called me a few minutes ago."

That stopped her cold.

"What? How?"

"He's safe. He wanted to let me know that."

"Why didn't he call me?"

"He asked me to let you know. He knew we've been in contact. He wasn't actually kidnapped."

"You're telling me he went willingly?"

"In a way."

This was getting crazy. "You're not making sense."

"Your father decided to take care of the Hungarian on his own. You see, he knows who he is."

She let her mouth fall open. "He does?"

Corbett's sigh sounded tired. "As do I. There's additional information I need to tell you."

She and Sean exchanged a suspicious glance. "New information?"

"Not exactly new. I thought Phillip would have told you by now, but he's a man of his word. He promised me years ago never to reveal what had happened. Some secrets can only be told by the person most affected."

Alarm bells went off in her head. "More secrets. Great."

Corbett ignored her. "As you know, your father and I share a history."

"Boyhood friends, best friends." She'd heard the stories all her life.

"Yes. But, when we were growing up, there was another." He cleared his throat, still sounding coolly collected. "There were three of us."

"Three?" She didn't understand. "All I've ever heard about were my dad and you. Corbett and Phillip. Best friends. There were only the two of you."

"No. There was another. We swore a vow, your father and I, never to talk of him or to say his name."

"But all the photographs I have show only you two."

"We destroyed all the others. But now, I'll break my own vow." Corbett sounded grim. "The Hungarian was the third. We were inseparable. Phillip, myself and…Viktor."

"Viktor?"

"Yes. Viktor was—is—my cousin."

"Are you telling me that my father is safe?"

"Not exactly."

Her temples were starting to ache. "Explain, please."

"Phillip went in to try to—as he put it—talk some sense into the Hungarian. He ended up being a prisoner."

She could barely contain her impatience. "Is he in real danger or not?"

"I'm not sure. Viktor has no reason to hate him, unless it's because he associates him with me. But my cousin's mental instability is a factor. Either way, before you make plans to try and rescue him, your father thinks he can handle this himself. He says he doesn't want you going anywhere near him."

"Of course he doesn't!" Natalie exploded. "But you and I both know I'm going anyway once I know where he is. Where is he?"

"He refused to tell me."

Natalie wondered again if Corbett was telling the truth.

"What are his reasons?" Sean stepped forward, placing a cautionary hand on Natalie's shoulder.

Corbett sighed. "He has some crazy idea of trying to talk sense into my cousin. After all, we were all close friends once."

"What happened to change that?" Natalie asked.

"Now is not the time—"

"Yes, it is. Now more than ever before, we need to lay all our cards on the table." She shot Sean a meaningful look. Narrowing his eyes, he shook his head.

Corbett coughed. "I really don't think—"

Ruthless, again she cut him off. "Neither do we. Now tell us what happened to make your own cousin hate you so much that he wants to kill you."

Chapter 10

Silence.

"A woman?" Sean guessed.

"Yes." Corbett's clipped reply told them he still found the subject unpleasant. Tough. "We all fell in love with the same woman."

Incredulous, Natalie met Sean's gaze. "All three of you?"

"Unfortunately, yes."

"She must have been some woman."

"She was."

Natalie swallowed as a thought occurred to her. "Please tell me this wasn't my mother?"

"No." Finally, Corbett chuckled. "This happened

a year before Phillip met Evelyn. One year, three months, and a few days, to be exact."

"You've never forgotten her." Sean made the question a statement. "Even after all this time."

"Phillip recovered first. Loving Evelyn helped him."

The nonanswer intrigued her. "What about you?"

"I barely remember her face."

Though she suspected Corbett was being less than truthful, she didn't comment. Instead, she tried to stick to the information related to the topic. "But Viktor still…"

"Who knows what Viktor thinks?" Corbett's usually civilized tone was laced with acid bitterness. "Obviously, he still wants revenge."

"For what? You still haven't told us what happened to cause the split between you three."

The strangled sound that came over the phone line revealed the depths of Corbett's pain. "She chose me."

"And Viktor didn't deal with this well?"

"No. Viktor had a psychotic breakdown. He raped and killed her."

Shocked, Natalie and Sean locked gazes. "He what?"

"He raped and killed her and then blamed me for her death." Clearing his throat, Corbett made an obvious effort to regain his composure. "I went to the police, but Viktor had disappeared."

Natalie wanted to ask how and why, but Sean, apparently reading her mind, shook his head.

"Now that you know the past," Corbett continued. "How will that knowledge help with the present? Viktor has your father, my closest friend. And Phillip somehow believes he can talk sense into a madman."

Sean's expression revealed how stunned he was by Corbett's news, though his steady voice gave away nothing. "Surely you have an operative in place who can help us?"

"SIS might be a better source."

Natalie shook her head. "No. I'm not contacting them. Until the mole is captured, I can't trust anyone."

"I understand. Let me make a few phone calls and see if I can set up a meeting."

"Just warn your guy," Sean spoke up. "Have him take precautions. We don't want another one of your operatives to wind up dead."

Corbett agreed, promising to phone them back once he'd arranged a meeting.

While they waited for his call, Sean went out for more food while Natalie continued working on the laptop. When he returned a few minutes later with a packet of freshly made roast-beef sandwiches, she put the computer aside. In silence, they devoured the food, washing it all down with warm root beer.

Corbett called a few minutes after they'd finished.

"I've got someone working on it," he said. "My operative is trying to arrange a meeting for you with one of his sources. The guy's been claiming to know where the Hungarian is holed up. If he talks, he'll want cash for the information."

Cash. The one thing they were short of.

"We don't have any—"

"I do," Sean interrupted. "How much do you think he'll want, Corbett?"

"Depending on who you speak with, it could be anywhere from eight hundred euros to eight thousand."

Sean whistled. "High-priced informants you got there, don't you think?"

"Not for the kind of information we're wanting."

"Corbett?" Natalie heard the tremble in her voice and realized she was perilously close to tears. "If you hear anything else about my father—or *from* my father, please let me know."

"I will."

Natalie disconnected the call and turned away from Sean, not wanting him to see her cry. If she'd ever viewed the world through rose-colored glasses, those had cracked piece by piece, finally shattering with the knowledge that even her own father had lied to her by omission.

She'd nearly made it to the bathroom when Sean grabbed her and wrapped his arms around her. As she started to fight him, the dam broke. She cried, her sorrow fueled by frustration and rage. She grabbed his shirt with both hands, holding on as though she might be swept away by the flood of her emotions if she were to let go.

"Damn you all to hell." And she yanked him to her, pressing her mouth against his.

Shocked, Sean couldn't move. Couldn't think, couldn't breathe. But this was Natalie. Natalie. Kissing him, touching him, *of her own free will.*

Shock gave way to disbelief, disbelief to pleasure. He tried to hold back, but the sweet sweep of her tongue inside his mouth made him dizzy and hot.

But why? Though he wanted to take it further, first he had to know.

He pulled back, unable to resist rubbing nose to nose with her the way they used to do. "Nat?"

She understood without him asking, as he'd known she would. She took a deep breath, meeting his gaze, her own dark with passion.

"I hate you for what you did."

Part of him understood. "Only a thin line separates hate from love."

"True." Pressing her lips to his jaw, she touched his shoulders, sliding her hands down his arms. "As it does anger and passion."

As badly as he wanted her, he didn't want it like this. "Not the first time we come together. Not in anger or revenge. I want it to be more."

"More?" She shook her head. "I could convince you, you know. I still remember everything you liked."

"You could, but you won't."

She went still. "How do you know?"

"Because I've wanted to make love to you since day one. I could have coaxed you into it a hundred times." His voice deepened as he remembered. "I've forgotten nothing, Nat."

She started to speak, but he shushed her with a finger against her lips.

"I've missed you so damn much. Even though us being apart was my fault, all my fault, I want you to know that not a day went by without me thinking of you. Missing you. Wanting you."

Her chin dipped. When she raised her head, the shimmer of tears mixed with the passion lingering in her eyes. "I've missed you, too," she murmured. Her words, the lush softness of her voice, felt as much like a caress as her soft hands. "When you…died, you left a hole inside me. Everything was off balance, nothing felt right. Even the everyday things, like drinking my morning cup of coffee without you to share it with, were unbearable because they made me think of you."

Her voice caught, but she continued. "Your arm around me, your breath against my cheek. The way you liked to sleep, spooning close behind me."

Low in his throat, he made a sound, a cross between a groan and a growl. She continued to touch him, tentatively at first, then with growing boldness.

"Make love to me, Sean."

"For old times' sake?"

"For that and…for the times yet to come."

At those words, she reached up to pull him to her, but he met her halfway. Slanting his mouth over hers, he drank her in deeply, wanting to believe, needing to believe, with his body as much as his soul.

He hadn't dared to think of the possibility of a future between them, nor did he dwell on it now. She wanted him, and not out of frustration or anger. Whatever complicated emotions drove her were most likely emotions that he'd felt.

Mouth to mouth, he tore at her clothes, shuddering as she used her fingers to pluck open his buttons.

Naked, he pressed his bare skin to hers, wanting all of her, more of her. His arousal pressed against her belly, and she gave him a smile of invitation. Taking his hand, she led him to the bed, sinking down into the soft comforter and holding her arms out in welcome.

Slowly, slowly. He knew it would take every bit of his self-control not to rush things. Still, he fought against the urge to take her with savagery until they were both mindless with passion.

If he was lucky, that would come later. For now, he'd go slow and savor her.

"Please," she whispered. Odd how one word, uttered so softly, could almost undo him. "Please," she asked again. And he complied.

When he entered her, the sense of *rightness* nearly made him weep. Finally, at long last, he'd come home.

Forget the cottage in the Highlands with its drafty walls and remote, wild fields of heather.

This was where he belonged. Inside her, wrapped around her, arms and legs tangled together. Skin to skin, scent to scent.

One look in her eyes and he knew she realized it, too.

He wanted to devour her.

"I want…" Her eyelids drifted closed.

"This?" He moved inside her, watching her expression go from dreamy to a sort of urgent hungry passion.

"Yes, this." Smiling seductively, she clenched her body around him, squeezing him with such exquisite sensation that he gasped.

"Ah, this." The internal caresses swept away whatever fragile control he'd been able to maintain. He drove himself into her, deep and hard and furious, straining to possess her, even as he knew she already possessed him.

Natalie, Natalie, Natalie. His wife, the other half of his soul.

She cried out, her cry dwindling into a moan. Nearly delirious, he answered her, struggling to keep from finishing too early.

"Don't move," he ground out, and he held her still, groaning when she squirmed against him, finally giving up the fight and letting the barely contained beast inside him free.

She met him thrust for thrust. As their bodies moved together, more than physical sensation passed between them. Lovemaking had always been like this between them, raw and heady, sensual and cerebral.

For him, there was no other.

When he could hold himself back no longer, when he poured his essence into her, he gave her all of himself. Emotion, love—everything she'd been to him, always would be to him—he laid bare before her. His heart on a silver platter. His body, hers to arouse. And his soul, shivering in the palm of her hand, for safekeeping.

If only she'd realize the truth before it was too late.

Still holding Natalie, Sean drifted in and out of sleep. His cell rang, instantly bringing them both awake in the early-dawn light.

Caller ID showed Corbett's number. Sean answered on speaker.

"My operative found someone who may be helpful." As had become his habit lately, the older man didn't bother with pleasantries. "He's agreed to meet with you. He claims he has key information for deciphering the code."

Sean glanced at Natalie, holding up a finger in warning. "That's not enough. We need more. Find someone who knows how to get in contact with the Hungarian. I have a message I want to deliver."

"A message?" The normally unflappable Corbett sounded surprised. "What kind of message?"

"That's between me and him."

Corbett cleared his throat. "Come on now, Sean. You're not about to try something foolish, are you?"

Before Sean could respond, Natalie spoke up. "What about my father? Have you heard anything else from him?"

"Nothing."

The loud sigh showed Natalie's feelings. "I'm worried. I don't like him being involved in this at all. I'd like to get him out of there before the shooting starts."

"Shooting?" Sean could picture Corbett's raised brows. "What are you planning?"

"Nothing." Her impatience came through loud and clear. "But you never know. Sometimes a hail of bullets is the only way to get inside. We can never predict what might happen."

"I understand." And Corbett did. He'd done his own share of fieldwork over the years. "But I'm quite certain your father is safe for now. I would have heard if he wasn't."

"You think so?"

"Definitely. The Hungarian would have wasted no time. He knows how much Phillip means to me."

"True," Sean agreed. "Still, I agree with Natalie. We need him far away from there before we go in. The possibility of him being used against us is too great."

"Of course it is." Again, Corbett sounded weary. "And I assure you I'm working on locating him. In the meantime, what would you like to do?"

"I want to meet with this informant." Natalie shot Sean a look daring him to contradict her. "I'm on the edge of cracking this code, which might be a fast line toward finding his location. Whatever information your informant imparts could be the key I need."

"Excellent. Do you have a pen?" At Natalie's affirmative, Corbett listed the details, his voice returning once more to its normal professional crispness. "Phone in once the meeting is finished and let me know the details, will you?"

"Of course." She punched the off button, staring down at the phone silently.

Dragging his fingers through his hair, Sean sighed. "What do you think?"

When she raised her gaze to his, the tortured look in her beautiful eyes made him want to comfort her. Since he knew she wouldn't welcome this, he refrained.

"Damn him to hell." Her low voice sounded fierce. "Going after me is one thing—it comes with the job. But my father? When I find him and get him out, that Hungarian is going to pay, I promise you."

Sean didn't tell her what he privately feared. If their enemy was as ruthless this time as he'd been when he'd cut down Sean's entire family, her father was already dead.

He crossed his arms. "Hopefully, this informant won't get killed."

She checked her watch. "We've got a little over an hour. How long do you think it will take to get there?"

"Thirty minutes, tops. Even in traffic."

"Then let's head out. I'd like to be early."

Outside, the damp drizzle and slate skies suited his mood. They drove into the city in silence, arriving at the agreed-upon meeting place—a city park—in good time. Parking, Sean took a deep breath, noticing how pale Natalie looked.

She got out of the car first, waiting for him to lock it and walk over to join her. The air smelled like moist dirt, as though the thirsty ground was absorbing the rain.

"Are you ready?" Hunching into his coat, Sean stole a glance at Natalie, who remained ominously quiet.

With a brisk nod, she surged forward, obviously wanting to walk ahead of him.

"Together," he cautioned, relieved when she slowed and waited for him to reach her side.

"You're right." She chewed her bottom lip. "I'm sorry. I'm worried about my father."

"I hope this guy will have some useful information." He kept his tone calm and professional.

"He's supposed to have a clue on the code. If I

can break that, we'll really have a worthwhile bargaining chip."

"If he's not lying." He sighed, patting the battered briefcase he carried that held the required money. "Informants do that occasionally, you know."

"Of course I know. Especially since this guy knows we're willing to pay his price. His info had better be good." Trudging into the rain, Natalie seemed not to notice the chill, or how leaving her head uncovered made her wet hair plaster to her scalp. She looked like a determined, drowning swimmer struggling to stay afloat.

He could only hope the analogy wasn't really accurate.

They slipped through the iron gate and into the deserted park. In the summer, the area would be brimming with tourists, but on a blustery autumn day, not even the locals ventured out.

If the bad weather was an omen…

"Not promising," she muttered. "Open spaces, with lots of trees to hide behind. If there's a sniper, we're obvious targets."

"This guy's an informant. He should be used to being careful."

"Maybe. But this is too much like the abbey."

Damn it, she was right. They could only hope this meeting didn't mirror the other.

"There," she whispered. "Straight ahead."

Near the gazebo, a man waited, collar turned up

against the rain. He wore a dark slicker and stood, head down, hands crammed into his pockets, pretending not to notice their arrival.

Not a good strategy for staying alive. Still, Sean cautiously approached, cursing his rapidly increasing sense of apprehension.

"Are there ducks in the pond?" Sean asked, using the prearranged phrase.

The man looked up. His eyes were such a bright blue they had to be colored contacts. "Ducks in the pond, ducks in the sky. They even fly in the rain."

The right answer. Still, Sean knew better than to relax. The informant, with his bright, darting eyes and facial tic appeared strung-out. His rumpled clothing and mussed hair indicated he hadn't slept in days. The musty odor emanating from him confirmed it. Meth addict.

Natalie moved closer to Sean. A reflex action, made without thinking, no doubt, but such a small thing pleased him.

The informant noticed. "I've been down for a while," he said, scowling. "This job ain't easy, you know."

Being a snitch *was* a difficult—and messy—way to earn cash. Only desperate men attempted to take on such a job. If word got out, death awaited. If you were lucky, they'd put a bullet in your head and you'd die swiftly. Not so lucky, and who knew what limbs they'd remove? Sean had heard of one informant who'd become an organ donor—while still alive.

No, being a snitch wasn't for the faint of heart. Most had a drug habit or some other overwhelming compulsion that needed feeding. From the looks of this guy, it was the same old story.

"What do you have for us?" Sean didn't bother to conceal the impatience in his tone. Sometimes junkies looking for their next fix tried to exchange false information or, worse, no information, for cash, then run.

No way in hell was he letting that happen. The stakes were far too high.

Perspiring profusely, even though the damp air carried a chill, the man held out his grungy hand. "Money first."

Right. "I'm not paying you until I see what you've got."

"Oh, all right." Instead of handing over information, the informant took off running.

Damn it. His gut instincts had been right.

"Setup!" Sean pushed Natalie to the ground, tensing as he waited for the sound of gunfire or an explosion.

Instead, there was only the gentle sound of the rain and the distant murmur of traffic.

"He didn't have anything." Sean didn't bother to hide his disgust. "If he was going to go to all this trouble, I would have thought he'd have had more of a backup plan. Either way, he's long gone now."

Ignoring his outstretched hand, Natalie struggled to her feet on her own. "Look." She pointed.

What he saw didn't really surprise him.

Their informant stood at the edge of the path, maybe fifty feet away, watching them. When he saw them looking, he crooked his hand, telling them to follow, and proceeded walking, back toward the business area where they'd parked.

"This guy's an amateur. He wants us to follow him. To where a trap awaits, no doubt. How much more obvious can he be?"

"But Sean, if they were going to spring a trap, this would be the perfect place for it." She waved her hand at the deserted park. "No witnesses, no innocent bystanders to get in the way. Maybe he's legit."

"And pigs can fly. Come on, Nat. You know better."

"Look, they have my dad." She set her chin in that stubborn way of hers that he knew so well. "I'm going to take any chance I can to find him. I'm following the guy."

"Fine." Grudgingly, he conceded. "But we keep a good distance between us and him and bail at the first sight of anything dangerous, agreed?"

"Agreed." She moved forward.

Keeping back fifty feet, they followed.

When they reached the sidewalk, they saw the man enter a small coffee shop.

They exchanged a look.

"What do you think?" Sean asked. "Do we follow him?"

"We have so far. We should be safe in there. And maybe he does have something useful to tell us."

"Somehow I rather doubt it."

"Me, too, but you never know."

"Let's go then." He took her arm and they crossed the street.

Once inside, they saw he was already seated, sipping from a paper cup of coffee. He motioned them to chairs.

"We'd rather stand," Sean told him.

He shook his head. "Not an option."

"Listen here, buddy," Natalie began furiously.

The informant opened his coat.

What they saw made them both freeze.

The man had been wired with explosives.

"That's right." He smirked, but there was no amusement in his face, only tired resignation. "So I suggest you do as I say."

If he triggered the bomb, he'd blow up not only himself and them, but everyone inside the coffee shop.

Of course, they couldn't allow this to happen.

"What do you want?" Sean asked.

The man looked at Natalie. "The code. Hand it over."

Maintaining eye contact, she looked puzzled. "What code?"

"Don't play stupid. We know you have it."

Just like that, she abandoned the pretense. "There are only three or four people who know about that. How'd you find out?"

"Looks like you told a snitch," he sneered. "Someone like me. Maybe you'd better take another look at your friends. Hand it over."

She spread her hands. "I don't have it with me."

The man actually snarled. "Then take me to wherever you've hidden it."

Sean knew that Natalie did have the flash drive in her backpack. And there was no way in hell he was letting her go off alone with this walking bomb.

"Give it to him," he told her, earning a sharp look of disgust.

The man looked from one to the other, finally settling his gaze on Natalie. "Better do as your man says. Unless you want me to blow this place sky-high."

Natalie didn't move. "Go ahead."

The man blinked. "What?"

"I said, go ahead. Detonate your bomb. I don't care. What I don't understand is why you didn't just shoot me and be done with it."

Good question. Sean crossed his arms, waiting. He knew there was no way she'd let this man take out so many innocent civilians. For now, he'd follow along with her plan, whatever it might be.

Goggling at her, the informant shook his head. "Are you crazy or what?"

"No, I'm not crazy. But I'm not giving you the info. So, either detonate your explosives, or not. I don't care either way."

The lie in her voice was plain to Sean, but the stranger didn't know her. Beginning to sweat, he looked at Sean.

"Talk some sense into her, man. You don't want all these people to die."

That remark told Sean that Natalie's plan would work. The informant didn't want to be blown to bits either.

"I'm guessing you don't want to die either," he said. "Come on, Natalie. Let's get out of here."

Together, they walked toward the exit. At the door, Natalie turned and faced the still-stunned man. "Tell whoever sent you that I won't be bullied."

The stranger followed them outside to the back alley, muttering under his breath. "Come on, man, they're going to kill me."

Sean shrugged. "Better than killing yourself. Go crawl back into whatever hole you came from."

"Wait." Natalie stepped forward. "Are those even real explosives?"

The man shrugged. "I don't know. They gave me six hundred pounds to put this thing on. Promised me another grand if I brought them the info."

"Where?" Sean demanded. "When and where were you supposed to meet them?"

Sweat rolling down his face, the man blurted out an address.

"I know the area," Natalie said. "Bad part of town."

"Of course."

"I don't get it," Natalie continued. "They only ask for the coded message. What good will it do them?"

"Maybe the Hungarian has his own code specialists."

Her eyes went wide. "Of course," she breathed. "That's why he doesn't need me. He must have already broken the code."

Chapter 11

Stone-faced, the informant said nothing.

"Tell them this. I know they need whatever part of the message I've got. I haven't cracked the code yet, but I will. And when I do, I'm going after whatever it reveals. If they want it, they've got to negotiate a hell of a lot better."

The man nodded and took off running.

Once back in the car, Natalie began to shiver. She didn't know why—she hadn't been that cold. But the steady rain had soaked through her coat, granting the chill easy access to her skin.

"I'll crank up the heater as soon as the motor

warms," Sean promised. "When we get back to the inn, you need to jump into the shower."

"And make it hot." She shivered again. "As hot as I can stand it."

His gaze darkened, but he didn't comment. Instead, he turned his attention back to the road.

Once back in their room, she took the first shower, careful to lock the door behind her. Only when she was dressed did she open the door.

"Your turn," she told him, toweling her hair. "All that warmth feels wonderful."

He nodded. When he entered the lavatory, he left the door ajar. As soon as she heard the shower start up, she gently tugged it closed. She hated that she had to force herself not to glance inside, knowing that the sight of Sean's naked, water-slicked body would be more than she could resist.

While Sean was in the shower, she called Auggie. He answered on the first ring, sounding unsurprised to hear from her. "I just got off the phone with Corbett," he told her.

"He arranged a meeting for Sean and I with an informant who turned out be working for the other side," she said to him, relaying the man's supposed bomb and his demand for the code. "I don't understand it, Aug. If they were going to go that far, why didn't they just take me hostage?"

"Or take you out, entirely."

"Exactly. All they would have needed was one man with a high-powered rifle."

"Have you told Corbett?"

"Not yet. Sean will probably call him when he gets out of the shower."

"Corbett's worried." Auggie coughed. "I'll tell you the same thing I told him. Lass, you're in grave danger."

She laughed, she couldn't help it. "No lie. Tell me something I don't know, Aug. That's part of the job. You know that."

"But this is different," he insisted. "It's personal. You need to get out."

"I can't. They have my father. Even if I wanted to, I couldn't back down now."

The silence on the other end of the phone stretched on so long she wondered if he'd hung up. "Are you still there?"

"Yes." He cleared his throat. "I need to talk to you, then. Privately."

"So talk."

"Not on the phone. Not about this."

It wasn't like Auggie to be mysterious and secretive. "The line is secure."

"Maybe. Maybe not. We need to talk in person," he insisted. "Our old meeting place."

Auggie had helped her keep her sanity after she'd lost Sean. They'd met weekly in an obscure little beer garden frequented mostly by students. As her sorrow grew unmanageable and SIS refused to let her return to work, Auggie had been the recipient of numerous late-night phone calls. He'd also been the shoulder she'd cried on during red-eyed coffee-shop meetings at the crack of dawn.

Literally, Auggie had become her best friend. She trusted him with her life. They'd continued their meetings, less frequently as time went on, but their beer garden had continued to be their favorite meeting place.

Until she'd quit drinking. Meeting in a beer garden wasn't conducive to staying sober.

If he said they had to meet in person, then they had to meet in person. But the beer garden?

"Auggie, you know I don't drink anymore."

"You drink hot cider, right?"

Breathing a sigh of relief, she nodded. Then, re-alizing he couldn't see her, she said yes.

"They serve that. No one knows about this place but us—no one. So we can't be followed or over-heard. Please, meet me there. This is important."

"When?"

"Tonight. And come alone."

"What time?"

"Normal time."

He *was* being careful. Normal time for them had been ten o'clock at night, which might work to her advantage. If she was lucky, Sean would fall asleep early. If not, ditching Sean before then would be damn near impossible.

"How about an hour later?" she asked, to be on the safe side. "I'm not sure I can make it before then."

After he agreed, she disconnected the call. Whatever Auggie had to tell her must be huge.

That night, after a big meal, Sean reclined in the overstuffed chair and turned on the television. "I don't want to talk strategy or even think about anything pertaining to the mission tonight," he warned her. "I need to relax if I'm to be on my game tomorrow."

Since that fitted perfectly with her strategy, Natalie agreed.

He fell asleep before the early news. Watching him, she suppressed the urge to brush a wayward lock of hair from his forehead.

Praying he didn't wake for a few hours, she slipped out the door to meet Auggie. Luckily, the inn was only a few blocks from the agreed-upon meeting place.

Once she reached the beer garden, she saw the proprietors had enclosed the garden for the winter, using clear plastic tarps over a huge, metal frame. Six-foot-tall patio heaters were situated all around the seating area, and several of the college students had removed their coats.

Taking a deep breath, Natalie stepped inside. The warmth was amazing. Heading across the concrete, she stopped in her tracks. Instead of Auggie, Dennie Pachla waited at the table she and Auggie had always snagged, two foaming mugs of beer in front of him.

Staring at the alcohol, Natalie nearly turned around and ran, but she trusted Auggie. If he wanted his friend the doctor here, then she would rely on his reasoning.

She continued forward, pasting a phony smile on her face while her stomach churned.

Standing as she approached, Dennie crushed her in a bear hug. "Ach, it's so good to see you, lass."

Natalie didn't waste time on pleasantries. "Where's Auggie?"

"He wasn't feeling well." He flashed a brilliant smile. "Must be a touch of the flu. He didn't want to stand you up, so he asked me to meet you, instead."

That didn't sound like the Auggie she'd talked to on the telephone a few hours ago. He hadn't been sick then. Nor had he acted as though he'd entrust whatever information he had to anyone else.

Something was up.

Yet Dennie was on their side.

Wasn't he?

Realizing he'd asked her a question, Natalie nodded. She'd always liked the handsome doctor and he'd made no secret of his attraction to her. Once, she'd found this flattering. Now, with her father in harm's way and the clock ticking, it was merely annoying.

"I don't have a lot of time," she warned, shifting from foot to foot, unable to hide her unease.

His smile faded as he searched her face. "What's wrong?"

"You shouldn't even have to ask, especially if you've talked to Auggie." Her uneasiness had reached epidemic proportions. "Look, maybe I should go."

Laughter erupted two tables over. One of the college-age boys pulled one of the girls down onto his lap.

Dennie stood. "Natalie, please. Sit down for a few minutes. We need to talk."

Reluctantly, she took a seat in the chair across from him, wincing as he slid one of the beers across the table. "No thanks. I don't drink." She glanced at her watch, wondering what the hell was going on.

He frowned. "Then why a beer garden?"

"Auggie promised me hot cider."

He laughed. "One beer won't hurt you. Believe me, I'm a doctor."

"No thanks," she told him quietly, knowing she needed to keep her wits about her. "I'm an alcoholic, Dennie. One beer to an alcoholic is like holding a match to a fuse. I can't risk it."

"Don't you want to test yourself?" Dennie continued to smile. "Go ahead and have the beer. It will relax you. I'm sure you have enough willpower not to have another."

You know you want it. The unsaid words reverberated inside her head. "I don't think— No." She crossed her arms. "No beer. I'd like some hot cider."

"Fine." He pulled her mug across the table to him. "I'll get you a cup of cider."

Perfect. As soon as he left, she'd call Auggie and find out what the hell was going on.

The instant he disappeared inside, she hit speed dial. Auggie's voice mail picked up. She left a brief message, then tried his home phone. Again, she got his machine. This time she didn't leave a message.

About to dial Corbett, she closed her phone and dropped it back into her purse when she saw Dennie approaching.

"Here you are." He handed her a tall mug of hot apple cider.

"Thank you." She took a tiny sip, almost purring at the taste. "Mmmm. This is good. So, how have you been?"

"I've been great. But Auggie's been so worried about you, I don't think he's been sleeping. That may have contributed to his illness."

He was lying and, worse, he sounded as though he was trying to make her feel guilty. Even more ill at ease, she scooted her chair around to place her back against the brick wall in a classic defense position.

"Why would he worry? He knows I'm good at what I do. I've been in tight spots before and I'll be in them again."

He nodded, smoothing his perfectly groomed hair. "I understand. But Auggie, he thinks of you like a sister. He says he can't help but worry."

She took a longer drink. The cider really was excellent. "Well, tell him to stop worrying. Seriously."

He grinned, but his eyes were still somber. "Auggie gave me a message to pass on to you."

Now she was really worried. She knew Auggie would never have entrusted something so important to anyone else. Especially since he'd insisted they talk in person.

Pretending nonchalance, she leaned back in her chair and took a long drink of the hot cider. "Okay. What's up?"

"It's about Sean."

Whatever she'd expected, it hadn't been this. "Sean?"

"Yes. Part of the reason Auggie is so concerned is because of the company you've been keeping."

"Sean?" she repeated. "Auggie knows all about him."

"Maybe, but do you?" His elegant eyebrows rose. "Word on the street is all about that husband of yours."

Gossip? She'd come here to discuss gossip? Though alarm bells were clanging loudly, she forced herself to remain seated and continue to drink her cider.

"Sean? I can imagine. After all, how many agents return from the dead?" Immediately, she thought of

Danielle, aka the Sparrow, and Mitch. Like Sean, both agents had returned from death's door. But Dennie wouldn't know them.

"Showing up alive after two years is a big deal, yes." Dennie didn't appear convinced. "But rumor has it that the Hungarian wants him badly. The bounty on your husband's head is up to four million now, and I've heard it's going up again." He watched her closely. "Some people will do anything for that much money."

Some people? People like him? Though she didn't understand why she was suddenly suspicious of a man she'd always trusted, she'd been trained to go with her gut instincts.

Her gun harness was within easy reach. For protection, she told herself. Pretending to scratch an itch, she unfastened the restraint and eased her pistol up enough to flick off the safety. If she was wrong, no harm done. And if she was right…she'd be saving both her life and Sean's.

"Do you have any idea how powerful this Hungarian fellow is? Can he really come up with that kind of money?"

Was this a game? Dennie knew enough about the intelligence community to be able to answer that himself.

"Of course he can."

"Wow. Four million. And there's something he wants even more than Sean."

She froze. "What's that?"

"A massive diamond. Called the Opar. I've heard it's hidden, and there's a coded treasure map."

The code. How did he know about the code? Unless Auggie had told him, and she didn't see the other agent doing that.

"Really?" Though her heartbeat kicked up a notch, she did her best to sound unaffected.

Dennie leaned forward, still staring. As she took another sip of her drink, she realized he hadn't touched his beer.

Damn. The alarms became a shriek of warning. She placed her mug back on the table, vowing not to touch it again until he drank.

She blinked as his image blurred, then came sharply back into focus. Rubbing her temples, she felt a headache beginning. "How do you know so much about all this, Dennie?"

He laughed, the sound seeming to come from a great distance away. "You might say I lead a double life."

A double life? Was he the mole?

"You're on our side, aren't you?" She spoke with great difficulty, slow and slurring. "Aren't you?"

He laughed, the sound echoing in her brain. "I want the code, Natalie. And you're going to help me decode it. That diamond's worth ten times the bounty on Sean's head."

The beer garden appeared to be spinning. Mouth

suddenly dry, Natalie licked her lips. "I don't feel so great. What's going on here, Dennie?"

If he answered her, she couldn't make sense of his words. Something was wrong—everything was wrong. She'd fallen into a trap and, despite her earlier promise to tell Sean anytime she made a move, she had no backup.

The instant he woke, Sean knew he was alone. Cursing, he clicked on the light and pushed himself out of the chair. He used the remote to turn off the TV, stepped into his boot cast and fastened it over the top of his jeans.

He'd fallen asleep in the overstuffed chair, and Natalie had gone...where?

The nightstand alarm clock showed eleven-thirty. A bit too late to take a stroll around the block, especially with assassins trying to kill her.

Where was she?

A look outside revealed she hadn't taken the car. He went to the closet, found her clothes still hanging in place. She hadn't taken them, nor her duffel bag. That meant wherever she'd gone, she hadn't gone far.

He headed out to do a search, intending to circle a five-block radius for starters. If Natalie was out there, he'd find her.

Forty-five minutes later, he'd begun to admit defeat.

Wherever Natalie had gone, she didn't want to

be found. He had no choice but to return to the inn and wait.

Somehow, he managed to fall back asleep. When he woke to a cold, gray drizzle, the other side of the double bed was still empty.

Immediately, he dialed Corbett's number.

"No, I haven't talked to her." Corbett sounded worried, which didn't bode well. "Have you tried Auggie?"

"You're the first one I called. The last time Nat tried to reach Auggie, she had to leave a message. He hasn't called her back, yet."

"That you know of."

Sean heaved an exasperated sigh. "Stop implying that Natalie's keeping secrets from me."

"Isn't she?"

"How the hell would I know?" Sean had to bite back his anger, knowing some of it still came through in his voice. "Natalie's missing. I don't know where she's gone."

"Or if she's all right," Corbett mused. Then, a couple of seconds later, he asked, "Did she break the code?"

The urgency in the other man's voice made Sean grit his teeth.

"No, she didn't break the code."

"That you know of."

"True." Corbett's suspicions wounded Sean. "But she would have told me if she had."

"Do you think so?"

"I do. She would have been excited, exhilarated. Natalie was never very good at hiding her emotions from me."

Until now.

"Maybe she'll show up." Corbett didn't sound as though he thought that was a likely possibility.

"Maybe." If she was still alive. "Give me Auggie's phone number, will you? I want to see if he's heard from her."

Once he'd written down the number, Sean rang off.

Dialing Auggie, he left a message on the answering machine asking for a return call. Then, because he'd never been a big fan of inaction, he got into the car and made another unsuccessful sweep of the area.

Then he went back to the inn to pace and wait.

When she woke in the backseat of the car, trussed up like a holiday turkey, Natalie's first thought was of Sean. She had made a mistake in not leaving him a message, telling him where she was going and whom she was meeting.

Her second thought was for Auggie.

"Did you hurt Auggie?" she demanded, glaring at Dennie in the driver's seat.

"Just a little." He didn't even glance at her. "Enough to knock him unconscious for half a day or so. He'll be fine."

"You're working for the Hungarian? I was under the impression you worked for us."

He didn't bother to answer.

"Why?"

"Personal reasons. He's making me prove myself before I get any real power." He smirked. "So far I'm doing damn good. If I can get that diamond, I'll be doing even better."

"How did you know I had a copy of the code?"

He laughed. "Auggie let it slip."

She took a deep breath, knowing she couldn't let loose and tell him what she thought of him. *Traitor* would be too kind a word. "What about my father?"

He did look over his shoulder at that. "Your father?"

Was he toying with her now?

"My father is with Viktor."

He wasn't able to hide his shock. "Why'd he take your father? What possible good could *he* do us?"

"He wanted to trade him for the code."

"And now he has you." Dennie seemed to find that amusing, chuckling to himself. "I'm one step ahead of him."

Natalie couldn't believe she'd once thought his aristocratic profile attractive. Now he looked arrogant and untrustworthy.

"But no code."

He laughed out loud at that. "Natalie, I know you.

You're meticulous. There's no way you'd let that data out of your sight. I'm betting you have it on you."

Instead of answering, she bit her lip. Though he was right, there was no way she'd give him the satisfaction of admitting it.

"Where are you taking me?"

"You'll find out soon enough. Enough talking." He turned the knob and cranked up the radio. Italian opera blasted through the speakers, making her head hurt more.

Not good. She needed to be her sharpest if she was going to face the Hungarian. Because, despite Dennie's lack of information, she had a good idea that was where he was taking her.

Wearing a path in the carpet didn't improve Sean's disposition. Sour stomach, sour thoughts. He popped a couple of antacids and checked his cell again to make sure he hadn't missed any calls.

The screen was disgustingly blank.

As he debated trying Auggie once more, the phone chirped. Caller ID showed it was Auggie.

"Talk to me," Sean said, answering the phone.

Auggie didn't waste time on pleasantries either. "Let me have Natalie. Please."

"Natalie's not here. She's disappeared. I was hoping you could tell me where I might find her."

The other man cursed. "I knew it." He outlined the details of the planned meeting between him and

Natalie. "He knew. He must have met with her in my place. I'm almost positive he's kidnapped Natalie."

"Who?" Please, God, not the Hungarian. "Who has Natalie?"

"Dennie Pachla. I was getting ready to leave to meet with Nat and Dennie came over. He must have hit me on the back of the head."

Dennie Pachla. Sean wished he could remember why the man had looked so familiar. "Why? What's his motive?"

"I'm not sure. But I'm willing to bet he's working for the Hungarian. I'm thinking he's taking Natalie to him."

Sean didn't have to ask the reason this time—he knew. "If you hear anything, please let me know."

"I will, but only if you agree to do the same."

Giving his promise, Sean closed the phone. Not only would the Hungarian have the code, he'd have Natalie. He would achieve two things with one fell swoop. He'd locate the treasure and gain his revenge on Sean.

All Sean cared about was Natalie. He was betting the Hungarian knew that.

Now that he knew what to expect, he couldn't contain his restless agitation. Someone would be contacting him soon. He was sure of it. Bait was completely useless without a target.

Once they'd given him a rendezvous spot, he could take action. He could only hope Natalie and her father were at the same location. Rescuing them both wouldn't be easy, but rescuing two hostages was something he'd done many times.

Only this was more than a routine day's work. These two hostages were more precious to him than life itself.

Chapter 12

Dawn had not yet arrived when they reached the elegant country house with the well-lit wrought-iron gates and a long, winding drive. Squirming in the backseat, Natalie's mouth was dry and her bladder full, but she refused to complain, knowing Dennie might use any sign of weakness against her.

Dennie spoke with someone in the manned guardhouse, and the huge gate swung slowly open, then closed behind them.

Light beamed from every window of the stone manor house. They pulled around the circular drive and parked under the portico. Two men—big bruisers both, most likely bodyguards—emerged from the house, opened the rear door and hefted her out of the car. One grabbed her under both arms, the other lifted her legs, carrying her between them.

She glared at Dennie, who only smiled.

Inside, the blast of heat made her eyes water. Her two escorts carried her across a marbled foyer and down a long, ornately carpeted hall. They deposited her in a room she could only describe as something from an S and M aficionado's wet dream.

This must be the torture chamber. Duh. Scattered around the room were all sorts of medieval-looking devices, most of which she couldn't even identify or imagine a purpose for.

Unfortunately, she had no doubt she'd find out soon enough.

The guards dumped her on a wooden benchlike thing that could have been a rack—or some sort of pagan altar. After checking to make sure her bonds were still tight, they left without a word, closing the door behind them. She heard a sharp click and realized they'd locked her in.

She had no idea how long she had before the Hungarian arrived, but she wanted to take advantage of her time.

After struggling to a sitting position, a quick glance around told her the room had no windows. Even if she could move fast enough, there was no way to escape other than the door.

As she contemplated her admittedly limited

options, she heard a click and the door swung open. A tall, balding man in a dark suit entered the room.

Corbett's cousin, Viktor.

She took a closer look. Though heavier, the man known as the Hungarian had the same aristocratic nose and similarly shaped eyes as Corbett. He was tall and well-dressed, though his once athletic body was beginning to run to fat. The bronze tone of his skin told of his vanity; the color was not the same as a natural tan. A whiff of strong, expensive cologne reached her, making her struggle not to sneeze.

"We finally meet." His Hungarian accent made his speaking voice seem cultured, though the diction was rougher than Corbett's refined and British way of speaking. "My son has brought me the ultimate gift."

She couldn't hide her shock. "Your son? Dennie's—"

"Mine." He beamed. "And he's proven his fitness as my heir."

Filing away the information, she nodded. "What do you want with me?" she asked, although she already knew the answer.

His smile told her he was aware of this. "Come now, Ms. Major. Don't play the idiot blonde, or now, since you've changed your hair color, redhead. You know perfectly well why I've captured you."

"To lure Sean in."

"Very good." He rubbed his chin. "And?"

"And you want the code."

"No."

His answer stunned her. "No? What do you mean?"

"I *wanted* your data, when my people were working to break the code. I believed your message had some information that was missing from mine."

"Believed? Past tense?"

"I have the diamond. One down, two to go."

"Two? Once you have Sean, what's left?"

"Corbett."

"Your cousin?"

Brows raised, he looked surprised. "He told you? I thought he never talked about me."

"Oh, he does, all the time," she lied. "I think he misses you."

He slapped her, hard. "Liar." His spittle sprayed her cheek. "Corbett hates me, the same as I hate him."

Knowing she'd better change the subject fast, Natalie inhaled. "Now that you have me, what do you plan to do with me once Sean arrives?"

"Concerned for your pretty neck? You needn't worry—you're going to die."

"How nice," she murmured, not bothering to hide her sarcasm. "And what of Sean? What are you going to do with him?"

His answer was exactly as she'd feared.

"He will suffer." Viktor waved a pudgy hand

around the cluttered room, a huge diamond ring flashing. "Before he dies, he will regret what he's done to me."

"You want to make Sean suffer, don't you? Think how much agony my death would cause him if you killed me in front of him and then forced him to live with the knowledge that he couldn't save me."

He scoffed. "You're only a woman. He would get over it quickly enough."

"Ah, but he loves me. I don't think he would. He loved me so much he gave up his life, pretending to be dead, all to save me." As she spoke, suddenly she realized it was true. Sean had acted out of love, not out of whatever misguided motive she'd suspected.

He'd tried to save her, to spare her the exact fate she faced now. Because he'd loved her. He'd always loved her.

Now, her turn had come to do the same for him.

Her throat ached as she fought tears. Damned if she'd cry in front of her enemy. Then, as she realized they might help her plead her case, she let them flow.

The older man's eyes narrowed as he considered her words. "You might be right," he said slowly. He laughed, then rounded on her, his face contorted with fury. "What did you think I planned, you stupid woman? To kill you cleanly and then simply tell him you were dead? Where's the fun in that?"

Her heart sank as his rant continued. "After I capture him, I will torture you in front of him,

maybe let a couple of my men sample your charms."
He leered. "Then you will die slowly, while he's
chained and helpless to stop us."

Her heart skipped a beat, but she kept her gaze
steady. She would not panic. Trained agents did
not feel trepidation. She would be ruthless, do
what she had to do to save the man she loved.
He'd been willing to die for her once. She could
do no less for him.

"Fine," she said, her voice steady. "Do what you
have to do."

"I will, I promise you." His chuckle turned into
a cough.

She took a deep breath. "But once I'm dead, you
could release him instead of killing him. But not let
him have my body. Just tell him you fed it to the
crows or something like that."

Holding her breath while he considered, she
knew if Viktor accepted, Sean would never
forgive her if he learned what she'd done.
Offering herself to save him would be the last
thing he'd want. He'd suffer a thousand hells believing he'd failed his wife.

But he would live. That was all that mattered.

"I want him dead," Viktor roared. "Why would I
let him live?"

"Suffering, Big V." Drawling the words slowly,
she leaned in as though speaking in confidence. "If
you kill him, you end his suffering. If you let him

live, imagine how much he'll suffer knowing he let me down."

Viktor stared. "You may be right," he said slowly.

"I know I'm right." She put all the confidence she possessed into her voice. "I know Sean."

Rubbing his hands together, the older man stared off into the distance. "It's an interesting idea—to watch him suffer and then set him free so he can continue to suffer…yes. I think it's a very good idea."

She'd saved Sean. Breathing a sigh of relief, Natalie knew she didn't dare relax. There was one more person she needed to save. Her chest ached as she realized the Hungarian had said nothing about her father.

"Where is my father?"

"Phillip?" The beefy man stared at her, then chuckled. "Ah, something else you care about besides that husband of yours, eh?"

Lifting her chin, she met his gaze. "Where is he?"

"In a safe place."

"Let him go. You don't need him anymore. You've got me."

Shaking his head, Viktor rubbed the back of his neck. "One thing you learn in this business. If you want to survive, always have a backup plan. Your father stays put until I'm done."

"And then?"

He lifted one shoulder in an elegant shrug. "I

either let him go or I kill him. I haven't decided, though I'm leaning toward a clean sweep." He chuckled again. "Imagine that, all of them dead. Sean, Phillip, Corbett and Kitya."

Her heart sank. "You grew up with Phillip. He's done nothing to you. Let him go."

Instead of answering, he smiled. His expression was so ruthless, a chill ran down her spine.

"I'll send a message guaranteed to bring Sean to me. Once he's here, the fun begins." His echoing laugh was right out of an old B-horror flick.

When he left, he locked the door behind him, keeping her captive.

Again, she began working at her bonds.

Corbett called exactly four hours after Sean's last conversation with him.

"I got another e-mail." His voice sounded tight. "Asking for your cell phone number. It says if you ever want to see Natalie again, you'll tell me to give it to him."

Without hesitation, Sean gave his permission. "I've been expecting this."

"Have you? In a way, I have, too. But part of me has believed our Natalie would manage to escape."

Our Natalie. Sean liked the sound of that. "Me, too," he admitted. "But she hasn't, so I've got no choice but to go and rescue her."

"You make it sound as though you're the

cavalry when in reality you're more of a sacrificial lamb."

"Hey." Sean tried to make his tone light. "I'm never a lamb. Nor do I plan to be a sacrifice. I'm going in there and getting both Natalie and her father out safely."

"And if you don't?"

"If I don't, then Natalie will be a real widow this time."

"I'll reply to the e-mail then. Be careful, Sean."

Giving his promise, Sean disconnected the call.

His cell phone rang again twenty minutes later.

"McGregor here."

"Very good, very good."

He didn't recognize the voice on the line. "What do you want?"

"You. The Hungarian wishes to discuss your wife with you in person."

"Of course he does." His voice sounded calm, the voice of a man who didn't give a damn. Only he did, much more than he wanted any of his enemies to know. "When and where?"

Carefully writing down the directions, Sean ended the call as soon as he'd finished. Though the caller had given him instructions to arrive at ten the following morning, he meant to leave now and arrive early.

Maybe he'd get lucky and the element of surprise would be on his side. He was hoping they wouldn't expect him so soon. From the directions, the Hungarian's house was in the county south of Edinburgh, in the Pentland Hills. Not a bad drive if traffic was light. At this time of the day, he shouldn't have any problems.

The mansion was surprisingly easy to locate, though a drive past the immense wrought-iron fence revealed that the place looked impenetrable. He detected multiple cameras perched in trees just inside the fence, along with decorative spotlights that appeared to light up the trees but were actually sophisticated motion detectors. He'd seen them before.

They'd detect him ten seconds after he scaled the fence, assuming he succeeded.

But he had to try. Natalie needed him. After all, he had nothing to lose but her.

Of course the alarms went off exactly as he'd predicted. Since he knew running would be futile, Sean stood in the open with his hands raised over his head and let them capture him.

He didn't expect the blow to the jaw the first guard threw, nor the kicks to the stomach and back that followed once he was on the ground.

Writhing in pain and knowing he didn't dare to defend himself, Sean wiped the blood from his face and bit the inside of his mouth to keep from groaning. He let them haul him up then followed docilely into the manor house, keeping his wits about him.

If the Hungarian was here—and he bet he was—

his hired thugs were making sure not to leave Sean the slightest vestige of dignity.

Which was fine with him. That would make it easier for Viktor to underestimate him.

They tied his arms and legs together then deposited him inside a darkened, musty room that appeared to be an unused storage area. The musty smell, combined with the intense heat blasting from the vents, made Sean feel nauseous.

"You decided to arrive a bit early, did you?"

Though the dark room made seeing details difficult, when the tall, broad-shouldered man stood, Sean had an immediate sense of déjà vu.

If life was indeed a circle, then he'd managed to come back around to where he'd started. Face to face with the man who had destroyed his life.

"Early? I suppose I did," he responded, tamping down the rage-filled hatred that made him want to kill Viktor with his bare hands.

"Finally." When the older man spoke, he radiated confidence and power. Now, all these years later, knowing the truth, Sean saw how Viktor resembled Corbett.

And, he realized with dawning horror, Dennie Pachla.

"Dennie's, what, your son?"

With casual nonchalance, Viktor lit a cigarette, never taking his gaze from Sean. "Yes. Pachla is his middle name."

Clenching his hands into fists, Sean nodded. "I can't believe I never knew you and Corbett are cousins."

"Corbett *has* been talking." Viktor inclined his head. "You might have noticed the resemblance sooner if you'd seen the two of us together." He gave Sean a speculative look. "Does he know what I'd asked you to do for me? Did you ever tell him?"

"No. I didn't."

"Pity." Viktor smiled, a flash of blindingly white teeth, even in the dim light. "You failed me. And double-crossed me. For that, you'll pay."

"I already have."

"Not enough," the Hungarian spat. "Not nearly enough."

"More than enough." Sean could not contain his rage, nor did he want to. "Don't you think I've already paid? You murdered—no, you *slaughtered*—my entire family."

The older man actually smiled. "Yes. I thought that would be enough, but it wasn't. Maybe because your wife wasn't there. Then you pretended to die in that car crash. Took all my pleasure away, since I wanted you to suffer. When you resurfaced, once again you proved you weren't finished messing with me."

Taking a deep breath, Sean kept his voice mild. "But since you hold all the cards right now, you're calling the shots. I'm guessing you're going to kill me."

"Guess again." Eyes narrowed, Viktor exhaled another cloud of smoke. "Instead of doing what I asked, you changed sides and went to work for the Lazlo Group. You killed Kitya, too, which proved I should have taken you out for the first offense. I kept hoping you'd realize you'd chosen wrong, but you never did. I've waited a long time to make you pay for everything. Patiently waited. You deserve to die, Sean McGregor, but I'm going to let you live."

"You should know I didn't kill Kitya deliberately." Steering the conversation back to the past seemed safer. "She stepped into the line of fire in the middle of a big bust."

"Yes," Viktor snarled. "Seizing my arms. Guns I'd already paid for. Those were my weapons, Kitya got them for me. Your people had no right to take them. On top of that, when she died I didn't even know she'd stolen the diamond. I lost both the gem and my guns, thanks to you."

How well Sean remembered that day. There had been enough artillery in that shipment to arm a small militia.

"Tell me, what were you going to do with that many guns?"

"Take over another territory, maybe. If I keep it up, I'll own half of this country."

"But without the weapons…"

Viktor laughed. "Oh, I've already done it. Kitya wasn't my only source for weapons."

"What do you want?" The question had to be asked, though Sean already knew. In situations like this, certain formalities and rules had to be observed, at least with old-school gangsters like Viktor.

"You."

"You've got me. I'm here, unarmed, of my own free will."

"To save the woman?"

Since he saw no point in lying, Sean nodded. "Yes. To save the woman."

"She means that much to you?"

The question caught Sean by surprise. Before he could pretend disinterest, he knew something flashed across his face. A man as careful as Viktor would notice.

"She's my wife," he said.

Viktor coughed. "She told the truth. I wasn't sure, but you've confirmed it. Your woman—wife—isn't too bright, is she?"

Rather than bristle and attempt to defend Natalie's honor, Sean held his silence and waited, not sure where Viktor was going with this.

"Let her go."

He knew he'd been screwed when Viktor threw back his head and laughed. "She's going to die an excruciatingly painful death, right in front of you."

Sean barely suppressed his shudder. Wouldn't do to let Viktor know he'd voiced Sean's worst nightmare. "Let her go, Viktor. You've got me."

"Oh, I'm Viktor now, am I? Not Big V or the ambiguous Hungarian." He stepped closer to Sean, malice shining from his eyes and oozing from every pore of his fleshy, double-chinned face. "You worked for me, accepted my money. But when I sent you to kill Corbett Lazlo, you forgot all about our bargain. What makes you think I won't forget all about that?"

"That was ten years ago."

"So? The older you get, the more quickly time flies."

Changing the subject, Sean struggled to maintain his cool. "What about her father?"

"Phillip? What about him?"

"Is he still alive?"

"He's safe and he's resting." Viktor shrugged. "I don't know what else anyone could want."

Sean nodded. "Will you let him go?"

Viktor's gaze never wavered. "You are not in a position to bargain. Your Natalie wouldn't want that."

"Leave her out of this."

"Leave her out?" The older man chuckled. "Her thoughts for what I should do to you were perfect. I believe I'll take her suggestions."

"Let's just get this over with. But first, release Phillip."

Exhaling smoke, Viktor cocked his head, giving the impression he was mulling the suggestion over. "I don't know, Sean."

Instead of acknowledging that statement, Sean countered with one of his own. "You said he's all right. He's nothing to you now—not a bargaining chip, or a lure or even an instrument of revenge. He's a crippled man in a wheelchair. For Christ's sake, let him go. You have no reason to kill him."

"How well you think you know me." Viktor's smile vanished, replaced by a cold, arrogant look. "Do not mistake me for my cousin."

Not in a million years. Of course, Sean didn't voice that thought.

"You seem smug," the older man continued. "I wonder why?" He snapped his fingers and two burly bodyguards appeared in the doorway. "I can change that. Bring her in," he ordered.

Her? Sean tensed. A second later, his worst nightmare came true. Dread replaced rage as he watched them drag in Natalie and dump her on the floor at his feet.

Her hands tied behind her back, she appeared to be unconscious.

"No!" Sean snarled. "I'm who you want. You've got me now. Let her go."

Opening her eyes, Natalie raised her head and licked her lips. "No, Sean. That's not the way it's going to go down."

"Nat—"

"Listen to me." Her voice was low, cracked and

urgent. "I understand now. And once again, you're willing to sacrifice your life for me, though this time your death would be all too real."

Taking a deep breath, she continued. "But it's my turn to save you." She flashed Viktor a look. "My life for yours, this time around."

Her life for his. No way. No way in hell.

As he opened his mouth to tell her so, two guards seized him, dragging him next to her, close enough to touch if their hands were free.

When she met his gaze, her eyes were clear and free of fear. How was that possible? Didn't she understand what the man known as the Hungarian was capable of doing to her?

Maybe it was better she did not.

"What have you done?" he asked quietly, wishing more than anything he could hold her, protect her, shield her with his body, run with her until they were far, far away.

Viktor laughed. "You know, this is going to be fun."

"Fun?" Natalie rounded on him, her expression fierce. "What kind of man are you, that you find torturing and killing people fun? Psycho." She spat the word.

Sean inwardly winced. "Baiting the enemy is not the best idea," he said from the side of his mouth.

"I want to get this started."

Viktor walked over until he stood less than ten

paces from the two of them. "We will start in my own time." He scowled, glaring at Natalie. "And I'm not a psycho. There's nothing wrong with taking pleasure in vanquishing your enemy. I've won and I'll enjoy the victory and gloat all I want. And when I'm done…"

The way his black gaze swept over her left no doubt as to his intentions. Fury sweeping away rational thought, Sean tried to lunge for him, but his ties stopped him short and he ended up facedown on the rug.

Again, Viktor chuckled. The sound resembled Corbett's chuckle so closely that Sean raised his head and stared.

"What happened to you?" Natalie asked soft-voiced, her gaze riveted on the older man. "What happened to make you so bitter and hateful?"

Sean groaned. "Nat, stop. Goading him won't help us."

"Nor will it work." Viktor stepped around them, moving toward the door. "Everything will happen in my time, no sooner. And for the record, my dear, nothing happened to me. When I was a very young boy, I realized life was all about power. Whoever had it, had everything.

"My cousin disagrees, though he sought power in his own way. Life, death—all cycles we go through. The only thing that lasts is the legacy of power one leaves behind."

As the door closed behind Viktor and the lock clicked into place, Sean struggled to get up. He succeeded in rolling over so he was no longer facedown, but maneuvering his body up appeared impossible with all the ropes keeping him from any real movement.

"If they could see us now," Natalie said, a trace of wry humor in her voice. "A Lazlo Group legend and a Super-spy, trussed up like a couple of holiday turkeys."

He stared at her in disbelief. "You find the situation amusing?"

"In a weird way, yes. Sorry," she said, sounding anything but. "I've gotten everything I asked for—you and my father will be freed—and I feel like I accomplished my mission."

"The Hungarian never keeps his word."

"He will this time."

"How can you be sure? You don't know this man."

But Natalie, his Natalie, ever the optimist, looked at him through her rose-colored glasses and gave a weak smile. "This time, he'll keep his word. I've won."

He hated to keep at her, but Sean didn't see it that way at all. "Not until we're both free."

"I won't be leaving here. I've accepted that."

"He won't honor his part. How can you not see that?"

He didn't know what he expected her to say, but he wasn't prepared at all for the answer she gave.

"All I can do is try, Sean. You did the same two years ago. My life for yours. I've agreed to die so that you might live."

Chapter 13

"I won't allow it," Sean said bluntly.

"Really?" Mouth quirking, Natalie didn't know why everything seemed funny—maybe delayed shock—but it did. "And how are you going to stop me?"

He closed his eyes for a second. When he opened them, the raw agony she saw in his face wiped out any traces of amusement she might have had. "Sean…"

"No. I can't go on without you."

"I thought that once." She spoke as gently as she could. "But I survived. Two years I thought you were dead. Two years I made it one day at a time, without you. You did, as well, there in your hiding place in the mountains."

"That was different. I woke up every morning knowing you were still alive in the world, still breathing. Even then, my life wasn't easy, or fun. I missed you terribly. If he kills you…" He choked up and didn't go on.

He didn't have to.

She lowered her voice. "It will save you and my father. At least this way, we won't all have to die."

Shaking his head, Sean's mouth twisted. "Do you really believe that? He'll torture and kill you, and then he'll start on me."

"I did the best I could."

"No. No, you didn't." Expression fierce, he struggled again to get up. This time he succeeded. "In order to do the best you can, you've got to escape."

For the space of a heartbeat or two, she stared at him. Finally, she nodded. "*We've* got to escape. I'm not going anywhere without you."

"If we can somehow manipulate our bodies so that I can untie your hands and then you can untie mine, we'll have a fighting chance."

The doubtful look she gave him spoke volumes. "But our hands are tied behind our backs."

"What have we got to lose?"

"True." She backed up to him until they sat shoulder to shoulder. "Do you want to go first or shall I?"

"Let me." Moving his numb fingers as best he could, he finally was able to touch her hand.

"Try to get mine loose, Nat. They used rope on me and your fingers have much more freedom than mine."

Her tentative touch had him shaking his head. "Go for it, honey. You're not hurting me."

It took a good half hour, but she finally succeeded in working one knot almost loose. "Nearly there," she said, sounding as though her teeth were clenched. Even so, another endless twenty minutes passed before she gave a cry of triumph.

"Half of the first knot is loose. See if you can wiggle your hands."

The pins and needles were excruciating, but he had a lot more room to move once he tried. Just as he finished flexing his fingers, they heard the distinctive sound of the lock drawing back.

They both froze.

An instant later, the same two bodyguards entered the room. Stone-faced, they went directly to Natalie, each grabbing her under an arm.

"Where are you taking me?" she demanded. Sean tried to catch her gaze, wondering why she wouldn't look at him.

"Time to keep your promise," one of the men answered. "Viktor's waiting."

Though every instinct urged him to protect her,

Sean knew he couldn't. If only he had his hands free. "Don't touch her," he snarled.

The two ignored him, half carrying an unresisting Natalie to the door. An instant later, they were gone, locking the door behind them.

"Damn it." Sean set to work freeing himself, trying to complete what Natalie had started. His fingers were cramped and bleeding by the time he'd worked the first knot loose. The second and third were easier to untie.

Once his hands were free, he stuffed the rope in his jacket pocket, knowing it might come in handy later.

That done, he approached the door. Now all he had to do was figure out how to circumvent the lock and he could go rescue Natalie. This time, he knew she needed him. Handcuffed, there was no way she could get out on her own.

The guards herded Natalie down a long, polished marble hallway, shoved her into a room off to the right and closed the door quietly. Again, she heard the sound of the lock clicking into place.

Slowly, she turned, noting the fire blazing heartily in the stone fireplace and the heavy, gleaming cherrywood furniture. Full bookshelves lined the walls and two leather chairs made up a cozy reading nook in one corner, complete with lamps.

Viktor's library. Curious, she went to the shelves, reading a few of the titles on the spines. For a gangster, Viktor had eclectic taste in books. Anya Seton's *Green Darkness* had been shelved next to a dry military textbook. Interesting and confusing.

"Hello, my dear."

Viktor. Her shoulders tensed, but she forced herself to turn and look for him. She smelled the sharp citrus scent of his cologne before she located him sitting in another massive chair close to the fireplace.

"What do you want?" she asked, though she already knew.

"You wanted to be sacrificed…"

By the devil himself.

"I know," she said out loud.

"It's time to see if your word is any good."

"Not until you keep your end of the bargain."

"Not very trusting, are you?"

Instead of answering, she waited.

He sighed. "I only want to talk. For now. Please, take a seat."

Moving carefully, she crossed to the closest chair, sitting awkwardly, hating the way having her hands bound behind her back made her stick her chest out.

"How well do you know Corbett Lazlo?" he asked.

She had nothing to lose by being honest. "I've known him since I was an infant. He's like an uncle to me. He's my father's closest friend, which of course you know."

"Then you only know him in that regard? Family man, doting uncle?" He watched her closely. "You don't know the truth about him."

Truth? Maybe his version, but not reality.

"No. Since I've known him he's only owned the Lazlo Group. He was also my husband's employer."

Viktor's face darkened at the mention of Sean. "The traitor!" he spat. "He should have known I don't forget or forgive something like that. Killing his family didn't even begin to make up for what he did."

His skewed logic made no sense and she told him so.

"No sense?" Half rising from his chair, he appeared to think better of it and sank back down, glaring. "He betrayed me. I took him under my wing, taught him the tricks of the trade and when I gave him his first job, trusting him over any of my other operatives, he switched sides. Went to work for the man he was supposed to kill."

"Again, why do you want to kill your own cousin?"

"You don't know what Corbett did to me. He deserves to die. And your father, too, for taking his side."

Her blood ran to ice as Viktor continued. "All the people who betrayed me should suffer the same way I've suffered all these years."

Taking a deep breath, she willed herself to be

calm. "Does my father even know about whatever it is that Corbett did?"

"Phillip?" He waved away the question. "He's always been Corbett's puppet. He doesn't understand."

Persecution complex? She couldn't imagine anything Corbett might have done to this man—his own cousin—that was so horrible it warranted a death sentence.

"You think these deaths will make you feel whole again?" Guessing, true, but her statement was general enough that at least part of it should still apply.

"Yes." He nodded. "They have all got to pay."

"Why don't you tell me? Maybe I'm the only one in the dark, but I have no idea what you're talking about. What did Corbett do?"

For a moment, the arrogant mask slipped and she saw a hint of the person he'd once been. But only for a moment. Once he realized she'd seen, his expression went cold.

"Corbett ruined my life. He turned me in for rape. My own cousin!" He grimaced. "My own flesh and blood."

She didn't want to ask, but she had to know. "Did you? Rape someone?"

Narrowing his eyes, he appeared pensive. "Of course I did. I was famous for a few months that summer. Campus Rapist, they called me. All the coeds pretended to be terrified, but I knew the truth. They were secretly thrilled."

Bile rose in her throat. "How did Corbett find out?"

"That bastard. He had to know all along what I was doing. But he pretended not to. It wasn't until I went after his girlfriend that he decided to turn me in."

"You raped your cousin's girlfriend?"

Instead of answering, he gave her a smile so evil it chilled her blood. "And now," she said slowly, the awful dread making her chest hurt. "You're going to rape me, aren't you?"

His smile was all the answer he needed to give. As he slowly pushed himself up out of his chair, a loud crash came from out in the hall.

"What the…" Moving more quickly than she would have thought possible for a man of his size, Viktor yanked the door open. "Keep it quiet out there—" he began.

Something—or someone—crashed into him, pushing him back into the library and to the floor.

Natalie couldn't believe her eyes. *Sean*. With both hands free. She'd never been so glad to see someone in her life.

As Viktor floundered on the floor, trying to get up, Sean clocked him with a clean right to the chin. He fell back, hitting his head on the edge of the end table, and was still.

"Even with a broken foot." She didn't even try to keep the admiration from her voice.

Sean crossed to her and kissed her hard. "Turn around," he ordered, his voice hoarse.

Without question, she did as he asked. When he asked her to hold up her hands, she complied readily. "Did you find a key?"

"In the torture chamber room, he had dozens of handcuffs. And a huge key ring of keys. I might have to try all of them, but I'm willing to bet one of these will work."

She eyed the still-prone Viktor. "Let's hope you find the key quickly, before he wakes."

Luckily for them, the fifth key he tried unlocked her cuffs. Removing them, Sean massaged her aching wrists for a moment, before he turned and slapped the cuffs on Viktor.

"Let's see how he likes having *his* hands chained behind his back."

Rubbing her still-numb hands together, Natalie grimaced as the tingling pins and needles told her circulation was returning. "At least no one will come in and disturb us—they all think he's having sex with me."

The black look he gave Viktor told her what Sean thought about that.

"How'd you get out of the locked room?"

Sean's normal, confident expression returned. "I was a bit worried about that—"

"Just a bit?"

"Yes. But then one of those muscle-bound

bodyguards returned. I'm thinking he planned to rough me up a bit while everyone else was otherwise occupied."

She could well imagine what had happened. "He didn't know your hands were untied."

"No. And I waited until his back was turned before showing him. I don't even think he knew what hit him."

"What are we going to do with Viktor?"

"Let me call the local police." He grabbed the telephone and dialed zero for an operator. Speaking quickly and in a low voice, he asked to be directed to the Edinburgh Police Department. As soon as the connection was made, he explained the situation, told them he didn't know the address, and left the phone off the hook so they could trace the call.

This done, he walked over to Natalie and pulled her close. "We'll have to stay with him until the police arrive."

"Then we look for my father." She moved out of his arms, careful not to look at him.

"Of course. Someone in this place must know where he's being held."

"Maybe I should start searching while you wait for the police."

"Too dangerous. If they realize I'm missing or that Viktor's captured…"

It would compromise their position. So, as much

as she wanted to find her father *now,* she knew she'd better wait.

"I wish I had my cell." She patted her empty pockets. "We need to check in with Corbett and let him know what's happened."

"We will, don't worry. But I think we should call after we find Phillip."

Despite herself, she heard what he didn't say. *In case her father was dead.* She could only hope and pray he wasn't. Nerves had her pacing. "Agreed."

Though it felt like an eternity had passed since Sean's phone call, the clock showed barely thirty minutes had gone by before the police arrived.

Because they'd been warned, Edinburgh's finest surrounded the house, lights flashing red and blue, sirens screeching. Sean stepped out into the hallway, motioning with his hand for Natalie to stay put.

Feeling normal again, she ignored him, shouldering past him. "I'm part of this, too," she said.

He grinned. "Sorry. Old habits die hard."

From other parts of the house, doors were opening, people chattering in nervous, high-pitched voices.

"The household staff, most likely." Sean crossed his arms, still smiling. "I imagine the hired guns are waiting for their fearless leader to tell them what to do."

As if on cue, one of the husky bodyguards came

running around the corner. He skidded to a stop when he saw them.

While the bodyguard gaped, Sean pointed toward the long window at the end of the hall. "The police have you surrounded. The Hungarian is under arrest. You may as well give yourself up."

Moving his head in a jerky nod, the man started forward. As he moved past them, Natalie stepped forward.

"Wait."

When she had his full attention, she gave him her best sincere look. "If you can tell me where my father is being held, I can talk to the police about reducing your sentence."

"Your father?" He looked confused for a moment. Then, his expression clearing, he tilted his head. "The old bloke in the wheelchair?"

"That would be him."

"Talk to the police first," he said, a look of cunning creeping into his small eyes. "Once I have their assurance that they'll make a deal, I'll tell you what I know."

Though she had to grit her teeth, Natalie nodded. "Then wait here with us."

"What about Dennie?" Sean asked. "Do you know where Dennie Pachla is?"

"The doctor? He went home an hour or so ago."

A few more minutes passed before, finally, the

special team stormed in, clattering up the stairs with shouts of "Police! Put your hands in the air."

Natalie and Sean complied instantly. Until their identities had been established, they knew they'd be considered dangerous.

After a moment's hesitation, the bodyguard raised his hands, too.

In the chaos that followed, the team captain approached them. "We've verified your credentials." He held up a plastic bag. Inside were Natalie's tiny purse and Sean's ID.

After handing them over, he pointed to Viktor, visible through the doorway, still tied up. Two uniformed officers were trying to help him sit up. His eyes looked groggy and unfocused. "We've called for an ambulance."

"Good, good." Grabbing the now-handcuffed bodyguard's elbow, Natalie moved him over. "We need to talk to this man about a deal in exchange for some information."

After the terms were outlined, the captain had to call his boss. After what seemed an endless wait, he had approval to agree to the terms. A lesser sentence with possible probation if the information the bodyguard provided turned out to be accurate.

"They're holding your father in the abandoned Lachlan Mill about five miles up the road," the man said.

"Let's go." After a quick glance at Sean, Natalie started to leave.

"Wait!" The police captain called after her. "I heard this on the radio on the way over here. Lachlan Mill caught fire about a half hour ago. Unless a miracle happened, that place has probably burned to the ground by now."

Nothing but dry, rotted wood and sawdust, the mill was soon consumed by the fire. Even from a distance, Sean could see the place was an inferno.

His heart sank as they pulled up behind the line of fire trucks. It didn't look like any portion of the building had escaped the flames. Despite the steady stream of water the pumpers shot toward it, the roaring conflagration showed no sign of abating.

Natalie jumped out of the car and strode toward the blaze.

"Wait." Running to catch her, Sean grabbed her arm. "You can't go in there."

Her eyes were wild as she struggled to pull free. "My father's in there."

If Phillip Major *had* been inside that mill, he had no hope of being rescued now.

Natalie didn't seem to comprehend this. Again she struggled against his hold. "Let go."

He knew only one way to reach her. "*Agent* Major. Cease and desist. Use your training."

The commanding voice finally reached her.

"You're right." She went rigid, then her shoulders sagged as she heaved a sigh. "If I went charging in there, I'd get us all killed."

Did she understand? He wanted to hold her. Instead, he slowly released his grip on her slender arm. "It's all right. We all give in to panic now and then."

Panic. She made a face and he knew why. The word was foreign to a trained SIS agent. As a human being, however…they were all fallible. Especially when it came to loved ones.

Still, the second he released her, she lunged forward. "I've got to try."

He reached for her and missed. Damn it. Trotting along after her, he made one more attempt to make her see reason. "Natalie, wait."

"Wait?" She rounded on him, her expression spitting fire. "My father's in there. I've got to get him out."

Couldn't she see that the inferno had already consumed the entire building? There was no way anyone could get out now, especially a man in a wheelchair.

One look at her intense face told him she was willing to die trying.

He made a split-second decision. Better him than her. "Wait here. I'll go." He took off at a run for the blazing building.

A burly firefighter stepped in his path attempting to stop him. "Hey, buddy. You can't go in there."

"Watch me," Sean snarled, dodging him. Dashing around the back of what remained of the building, he searched for a place to enter. The entire back section had collapsed—its charred beams fed the huge fire.

Nothing remained of the mill but fuel for the flames.

Admitting defeat, he turned to go and nearly ran into Natalie. Her face showed shock and disbelief.

"Do you see him? Anywhere?"

The raw anguish in her voice broke his heart. "No." Gathering her close, he held her while she wept.

Her cell phone rang. She ignored it and didn't react when Sean reached into her purse to retrieve it and answer the call.

"Great news!" Corbett's exuberant voice sounded completely at odds with Natalie's broken sobbing.

"This isn't a good time." In a few sentences, Sean relayed the scene before them. When he'd finished, Corbett didn't respond. Sean guessed he'd want to do his own grieving privately, and said goodbye.

"Wait," Corbett sighed. "Is Natalie there with you?"

"Yes."

"Then walk her back to the front of the building. There, you'll find an ambulance treating smoke-inhalation victims. Phillip is there," Corbett told him. "One of my operatives is on the scene and called me. Phillip escaped before the fire got to his section of the mill. He isn't dead."

Without waiting to hear more, Sean shut the phone and touched Natalie's arm. Lifting her chin and making her look at him, he kissed her again, tasting the salt of her tears. "Come with me. I've got a pleasant surprise."

Later, after a joyful Natalie had been reunited with her father, who'd then been taken to the hospital as a precaution, Sean stood with his arm around her and watched the firefighters bring the blaze under control. She leaned her head into his shoulder and sighed.

Contentment? Or weariness? Sean didn't know which.

He wondered if she'd demand he divorce her now that they'd accomplished their objective.

The thought hurt more than he'd have ever thought possible. Whatever she decided, he still had some cleanup work to do.

Opening his cell, he punched in Corbett's number. The older man answered on the second ring.

"I've got something to tell you," Sean began, aware of Natalie listening and watching. "Before I came to work for you, I worked briefly for your cousin." His heart pounded so loudly he could barely hear his own voice.

Corbett went silent. Finally, after a few seconds, he cleared his throat. "Go on."

"He had me infiltrate your organization for the purpose of killing you."

"You didn't complete your mission, then." Corbett's cultured voice sounded amused. "And Sean, I knew all along that you'd worked for Viktor."

"You did?" Sean felt as though his jaw had dropped to the floor. "How? Why didn't you say anything?"

"How? I run one of the best intelligence agencies in the world, and you ask me how?" Corbett chuckled. "As to why I didn't say anything, I didn't need to. You made it plain where your loyalty lies. In all the time I've known you, you've never given me reason to doubt my decision."

Sean felt honored—and humbled. "Thank you."

"You're welcome. Now, when are you coming back to work here?" He meant the Lazlo headquarters in Paris. "Even though you've captured the Hungarian, I still have a mole inside the Lazlo Group. I'm still getting bizarre e-mails and I have agents being targeted. I need you."

"I don't know. That is…I…"

"Say no more," Corbett chuckled again. "Patch things up with Natalie, then call me. I'm hoping you'll both relocate here, if Natalie's willing to work for me instead of SIS. She'd be much closer to her father, too. I want to see you both wearing one of our black shirts with the green and gold plated pentagram."

"I still have mine," Sean said, feeling a bit wistful.

"Good, good. I hope Natalie will want one, too."

Sean eyed the woman he loved more than anything else in the world. "Wish me luck," he said. "I have a feeling I'm going to need it."

As soon as he closed the phone, Natalie turned and met his gaze. "You don't need luck." Her voice was soft and full of tenderness. "I understand now why you did what you did. I still think your decision was flawed and wrong, but you thought the same thing about mine when I made the bargain with Viktor to try and save your life."

"You never did tell me all the details of that bargain. What did you promise him?"

But she only shook her head. "Some things are better left unsaid. It's enough for me to tell you that in a moment of sheer desperation, I exchanged my life for yours, just as you did for me two years ago." She took a deep breath. "I love you. I can't—I don't want to—live without you. Promise me you won't leave me again."

He could scarcely believe his ears. Joy filled him. Joy and love and hope and the sharpest sense of gratitude he'd ever known. "You'll come back to me?"

"Yes." She brushed a kiss across his still-stunned mouth. "Just as you came striding toward me out of the smoke and the dust. You came back to me, Sean.

I'm never letting you go away again. 'Til death do us part," she quoted.

As he repeated the words, he felt complete. For two years, he'd lived his life as only half a man. Now, Natalie made him whole.

"We make each other whole," she whispered, as though she'd read his mind. Then she kissed him and he knew she was right.

* * * * *

Don't miss the next
MISSION: IMPASSIONED *tale,*
Kiss or Kill *by Lyn Stone, available December
2008 from Mills & Boon® Intrigue*

Mills & Boon® Intrigue
brings you a sneak preview of…

Caridad Piñeiro's Devotion Calls

*Ricardo Fernandez has the power to heal
people. But he also has one golden rule – never
get entangled in the private lives of people who
come to him for help. Despite this, Ricardo can't
avoid his attraction to Sara Martinez, a nurse
who has brought her terminally ill mother to
him for treatment. As the pair embark on a dark
adventure, could Sara use her own power to
heal Ricardo's heart?*

Don't miss this thrilling new story in
THE CALLING *mini-series, available next
month in Mills & Boon® Intrigue's new*
NOCTURNE *series.*

Devotion Calls

by

Caridad Piñeiro

Spanish Harlem, New York City

The saints' eyes followed him as he worked, scolding him for using them for his lie. Mocking him for denying the truth about what he was.

Ricardo Fernandez paused and laid his hands on the altar that embodied the fraud that was his life. All around him the statues of the saints condemned him. But he was used to such censure from those who refused to believe in his powers. Those whose fears forced him to hide behind the guise of a *santero*.

He looked down at his hands and, as he had countless times in his thirty years of life, considered why he had been chosen to carry this burden. Why these hands, which looked just like those of any other man, possessed the power to give life or take it away.

If he was a lesser man, he might have fallen into the trap of considering himself almost godlike. He might have opted to sell his abilities to those who paid the highest price to be saved. He could have even made a perfect assassin, able to kill without leaving a trace.

But Ricardo had done none of those things. Neither regrets nor revelry had a place in his life now, so he resumed his task. With a gentle touch, he removed the offerings he had placed on the altar the day before: the fine cigar, now just a half-burned stub and a pile of ashes, and the shot glass of fragrant rum, which had nearly evaporated from the heat of the radiator just a few feet away. After checking the water level in the vase of sunflowers he had placed beside one *virgencita,* he shifted to the last offering.

A small pile of coins lay at the foot of one statue. He gathered up the money in his hand and thanked the deity. While he himself was not a true believer in Santería, his customers held to this faith and he wouldn't besmirch their tenets. He hoped his prayer was deemed respectful enough by the deities that allowed him to use the powers with which he had been born.

Ricardo didn't like living a lie, but posing as a *santero*—a priest of the Afro-Caribbean religious

Santería—was the only way he could use his healing gifts. Many of the people who sought him out might not have come to him if they realized his abilities were earthly. They preferred to think the powers came from rituals beseeching their gods.

Of course, if some god hadn't decided to give him this boon, who had? Ricardo refused to consider the alternative, since he had sworn never to use the dark side of his gift. Not even when someone asked for it.

As had happened just the other day with Evita Martinez.

He had been seeing Evita for just over a year now, ever since the doctors at one of New York City's more prestigious hospitals had told her that there was nothing else they could do for her cancer. They'd sent her home to enjoy what was left of her life.

But Evita hadn't wanted to die just yet. Having heard about his unique abilities from some of the other ladies in the neighborhood, she had come to him for help. She and her daughter, Sara.

Sara, he thought with a sigh, recalling the way she had stood before him nearly a year ago, condemning him with her body language as he talked about what he could and could not do for Evita.

He knew that Sara hadn't believed him. Worse, that she considered him a charlatan. Her bright hazel eyes had skewered him with disbelief, much like those of the saints.

The disbelief in her eyes turned to trepidation when, after finding out that she was a nurse, he had asked for payment of a most unusual kind—blood. For a moment he'd thought she might run, and take her mother with her, but then despair had crept into her eyes.

Sara loved her mother, and at that moment she had been desperate enough to do anything to help her— even if it meant bringing bags of blood to a man she considered less than dirt. Ricardo hated relying on that despair. He hated the lying, but he did what he had to so he could help people.

When Sara brought a blood bag later today, he would have to tell the prickly nurse that her mother's cancer was growing faster than he could contain it, and that Evita had asked him to help her pass peacefully when the time came, rather than suffer with the pain.

Healing and killing. His gift and his curse.

A tap sounded against the glass of his door. He turned from the altar and stared toward the front of his store.

Sara Martinez stood there, her chin tucked into the thick collar of the charcoal-gray down jacket she wore against the lingering chill of winter. A crazy gust of March wind sent her silky shoulder-length brown hair swirling around her face. With a gloved hand, she combed it back and shifted from foot to foot, impatient and intractable as always about these visits.

The early morning sun played across her pretty,

heart-shaped face. She had a hint of a cleft in her chin, and hazel eyes that expressed so much with just a look. In his case, generally disgust. But he had seen how those eyes could warm to a molten caramel when they gazed upon someone she loved.

And her lips… They were full, at least most of the time. Not when she shot him a grim look, as she did right now as she waited at his door.

Drawing a deep breath, he prepared himself to break the news that would surely devastate her.

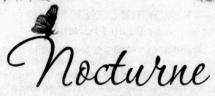

FROM INTERNATIONAL BESTSELLING AUTHOR DEBBIE MACOMBER

HIS *Winter* BRIDE

DEBBIE MACOMBER

Childhood sweethearts and unexpected romance...heading home for the holidays could lead to three winter weddings!

Available 5th December 2008

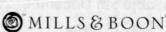

Celebrate 100 years of pure reading pleasure with Mills & Boon®

To mark our centenary, each month we're publishing a special 100th Birthday Edition. These celebratory editions are packed with extra features and include a FREE bonus story.

Plus, you have the chance to enter a fabulous monthly prize draw. See 100th Birthday Edition books for details.

Now that's worth celebrating!

September 2008

Crazy about her Spanish Boss by Rebecca Winters
Includes FREE bonus story
Rafael's Convenient Proposal

November 2008

The Rancher's Christmas Baby
by Cathy Gillen Thacker
Includes FREE bonus story *Baby's First Christmas*

December 2008

One Magical Christmas by Carol Marinelli
Includes FREE bonus story *Emergency at Bayside*

Look for Mills & Boon® 100th Birthday Editions at your favourite bookseller or visit
www.millsandboon.co.uk

FREE

4 BOOKS AND A SURPRISE GIFT!

We would like to take this opportunity to thank you for reading this Mills & Boon® book by offering you the chance to take FOUR more specially selected titles from the Intrigue series absolutely FREE! We're also making this offer to introduce you to the benefits of the Mills & Boon® Book Club—

- ★ **FREE home delivery**
- ★ **FREE gifts and competitions**
- ★ **FREE monthly Newsletter**
- ★ **Books available before they're in the shops**
- ★ **Exclusive Mills & Boon® Book Club offers**

Accepting these FREE books and gift places you under no obligation to buy; you may cancel at any time, even after receiving your free shipment. Simply complete your details below and return the entire page to the address below. You don't even need a stamp!

YES! Please send me 4 free Intrigue books and a surprise gift. I understand that unless you hear from me, I will receive 6 superb new titles every month for just £3.15 each, postage and packing free. I am under no obligation to purchase any books and may cancel my subscription at any time. The free books and gift will be mine to keep in any case.

I8ZEE

Ms/Mrs/Miss/Mr........................Initials ....

BLOCK CAPITALS PLEASE

Surname ....

Address ....

....

....Postcode ....

Send this whole page to:

The Mills & Boon Book Club, FREEPOST CN81, Croydon, CR9 3WZ